THE DESPERATE JOURNEY

"*Go up Jamaica Street*"

THE DESPERATE JOURNEY

Kathleen Fidler

Illustrated by Mike Charlton

CANONGATE • KELPIES

First published 1964 by the Lutterworth Press
First published in Kelpics 1984
Reprinted 1993, 1995

Cover illustration by Alexa Rutherford

Printed in Denmark
by Nørhaven AS Rotation

ISBN 0 86241 056 8

*The publishers acknowledge the financial assistance
of the Scottish Arts Council in the
publication of this volume*

CANONGATE BOOKS, 14 HIGH STREET
EDINBURGH EH1 1TE

CONTENTS

1. Davie crosses swords with the factor   9

2. The burning of Culmailie   27

3. Adventure on the road   43

4. The great city   59

5. A way is found   82

6. The trail to the Red River   106

7. The massacre at Seven Oaks   129

8. The land of promise   148

1. DAVIE CROSSES SWORDS WITH THE FACTOR

From the North Sea a keen wind blew over the shallows of Loch Fleet, where the river mouth widened. Always a wind blew there, as though it would force itself up and over the hills which lay in a half circle at the head of the Loch. David Murray bent to his task of mussel gathering. A hundred yards away along the shore his twin sister Kirsty bent her back too, and tried to fill her smaller creel.

David thought with satisfaction that, even when his father had taken what he needed for bait, there would still be enough mussels left over for his mother to make a good broth for supper. Suddenly Kirsty straightened herself and shouted to him, "Hi, come here quickly, Davie! There's a great partan under this stone!"

A partan! A crab! That was even better than mussels! "Where is he?"

"There! He's trying to sink himself in the wet sand under the stone. Oh, get him out quickly, Davie, or we might lose him!"

Davie seized a piece of driftwood and poked away under the rock, loosening the sand. One claw of the crab appeared, waving frantically, then another. Davie redoubled his efforts, scraping and poking. At last he dislodged the crab and brought it out.

"Stand ready with my creel, Kirsty!"

Kirsty lowered the edge of his creel as Davie pushed the crab towards it, then lifted it with the piece of wood in among the mussels.

"My conscience! He's a big one! He'll make a fine supper!" he exclaimed, turning the crab on his back so he could not easily crawl out of the creel.

The two children were so occupied with the crab that

9

they never noticed a horseman rein in his horse at the edge of the wood by the shore, tie it up to a tree-trunk, and make his way over the sands towards them. His feet made no noise over the wet sandy flats. His face became crimson with anger when he saw the creels filled with mussels, and he roared at the children in a voice of thunder, "What are you young rascals up to?"

Davie started and almost dropped the creel. Kirsty gave a cry of fear, and retreated a few steps. "Oh, it's Mr. Sellar!"

Patrick Sellar was the factor who collected the rent of their farm for the Countess of Sutherland, who owned their land.

"What are you up to?" Sellar repeated. "What do you mean by stealing her ladyship's shellfish?"

A spark of anger lit up Davie's eye.

"We're not stealing!" he replied indignantly. "My father has always had the right to gather mussels from the fore-shore for bait for his fishing."

"Right? He has no right at all!" Sellar shouted. "You know quite well these mussel beds are the property of the Countess."

"Indeed, sir, we do not!" Kirsty was bold enough to say. "How would my father fish for us if he could not dig bait?"

"James Murray's brats, aren't you?" Sellar said. "I might have known it! You are as impudent and full of argument as he is. I'll have no more of it. Tip those mussels back where you found them!"

Davie picked up his creel and backed away indignantly. Kirsty tried a little wheedling. "Mr. Sellar, sir, you would not be taking our supper from us, surely? Her ladyship will never be missing a few mussels from her grand table, now."

"Did you hear what I said? Tip those mussels out at once, or I'll do it myself!"

Kirsty turned to run away with her creel, but Patrick Sellar darted after her, snatched the creel and flung the contents into the shingle.

"Now, empty your creel too!" he commanded Davie. Davie glowered at him and made no move to do as he was told.

"Oh, please let us keep the partan, sir," Kirsty begged.

"No more nonsense! Do as you are told!"

There was a streak of obstinacy in David Murray which would not yield so easily. Besides, he felt he had right on his side.

"But we have gathered the crab and the mussels below high-water mark. My father says her ladyship the Countess has no right to shellfish taken below high-water mark, any more than she has a right to all the fish in the sea."

Patrick Sellar grew livid. To be defied by this strip of a boy was unthinkable! He advanced threateningly, lifting the riding whip which he carried. "Throw out those mussels at once!"

"I will not!" Davie stood his ground, though he went pale.

The whip flicked once and curled round Davie's bare calves. Stung to a pitch of anger by the pain, he snatched at the crab and flung it full in the factor's face. "Have your old crab, then!" he cried.

"You impudent young rogue! I'll flay the hide off you for this!" Sellar shouted, seizing the boy by the shoulder and lifting his whip again. The blow never descended, for his arm was caught by Kirsty, who swung all her light weight on to it.

"Let go my brother! Don't you dare to touch him!" she yelled, and, quicker than lightning, she sank her teeth in the factor's wrist.

"You young spawn of a witch!" the factor exclaimed, and he was about to turn on Kirsty too when he was stopped by a shout. A man was running towards them across the sand.

"What's going on here? What's to do, factor?" the man cried fiercely. "Are you lifting your whip to my bairns?"

The factor stopped dead. Kirsty rushed to her father.

"Oh, Father, Mr. Sellar hit Davie with his whip. Look at the red weal on his leg!"

"Is this true, factor?" James Murray's voice was grim.

"The lad's an impudent whelp. He needed a sharp lesson for flinging a crab in my face."

"That's not true, Father! Mr. Sellar struck me with the whip before ever I threw the crab. He would not let us keep the mussels we had gathered and the crab we had caught. He made Kirsty fling hers away." Davie pointed to the empty creel.

"You and your brats know well enough the shellfish on

the shore belong to the Countess——" Sellar began, shifting his ground.

"But we caught these below high-water mark," Davie interrupted. "*You* said everything below high-water mark was free for the taking," Davie reminded his father.

"The lad is right, you know, Mr. Sellar. That is the law."

"Who's to know where the boy took the shellfish, above or below high-water mark?" the factor muttered. "There's only the lad's word for it."

"My son is not a stranger to the truth. The Murrays are not given to lying," James Murray told Sellar with contempt. "Besides, it was well below high-water mark that you came on the bairns, here where we are standing."

"The law says all the foreshore belongs to the Countess," the factor insisted.

"Then I will go with you to the Countess and argue the matter before her."

"Think you I would take up her ladyship's time with so paltry a matter?"

"It was not paltry to you when you lashed my son with a whip," James Murray retorted. "If ever you dare to lift your hand to my children again, Patrick Sellar, you will have to reckon with me. I shall not let you off lightly." He turned to Davie. "Pick up the partan, Davie. It is yours. I know our rights."

Davie made haste to pick up the crab. The factor turned sullenly away.

"You are very free with talk of your rights and the law, James Murray," Sellar called over his shoulder. "Perhaps we shall see what the law has in store for you."

They stood still, watching him as he strode to the woodland and unhitched his horse.

"What did the factor mean by what he said last, Father?" Davie asked as the sound of the horse's hoofs died away along the road.

"No doubt we shall know before long. He is an ill man to cross."

"Perhaps I should not have thrown the partan at him, even if he did strike me first."

"Aye, Davie, better to keep a curb on your temper. This is a pretty kettle of fish in more ways than one."

"Why? What will Mr. Sellar do to us, Father?" Kirsty asked.

Instead of answering her, James Murray said, "Look! There's your mother at the door of the house." The children ran to her with the creel of mussels and the crab.

"Look what we've got! Look what we've got!"

"My! That's surely the grandfather of all the partans!" their mother laughed when she saw the crab. "A grand supper we'll have this night!"

"Let us hope it does not cost us too dear," her husband said in a low voice.

"What do you mean, James?" she asked quickly.

"I will tell you later when the children are abed," he said. "Not now."

There were two rooms to the small cottage. One had a fire on a rough hearth by the wall. Along the side-wall between the two rooms was a box-bed where James and his wife slept. The small room beyond was almost taken up by the children's two wooden beds. Built on to the end of the house was a shed which housed the horse, the cows and the few hens. The Murrays felt themselves rich because they had a horse. Many crofters had only a cow which they harnessed to a plough when they wanted to turn over the soil of the small fields where they grew their oats and barley.

The little croft was almost self-supporting, with milk and butter from the cows; eggs from the hens; smoked bacon from the pig they fattened and killed each year, and the salt mutton from the few sheep which also provided Kate Murray with wool for her spinning wheel. Kail and turnips and potatoes provided vegetables for the stew-pot; the oats, oatmeal for the porridge. On a quiet evening James Murray took out his boat to catch fish. The Murrays all worked hard on the croft and in the fields, but it was a happy satisfying life. The children herded the sheep and cows on the hill-side and helped their father to weed his small fields on the flat ground by the Lundie Burn, which ran past their door.

Behind their cottage at Culmailie rose the circle of the hills, Ben Bhragie steeply reaching away to the further ridge that stretched to Ben Lundie. Beyond there the hills rolled away in a gathering wave of peaks behind which the sun set. Always there was the murmuring music of the burn beside the house and the sound of the wind blowing off the sea. That was how Davie was to remember it in the troubled years to come.

When the children were fast asleep James told his wife of the encounter with Patrick Sellar.

"So that was what caused the weal on Davie's leg!" she remarked angrily. "I thought he had scratched himself on a briar. The factor should think shame of lifting his whip to a bairn like that!"

"Oh, Sellar did not get off scathless. Kirsty saw to that!"

"No one will touch Davie and get away with it easily if Kirsty is around. Born on the same day they were, and always one will fight for the other. That is how it will always be," she said with a far-away look in her eyes, as though she could see into the future.

"It's the *sight* you have, Kate," James remarked, with the belief of a Highlander that there are some who have the power to look beyond the present. "A good thing it was, though, that Patrick Sellar did not strike Kirsty, or I might have taken my fists to him. As it is, he will not let to-day's matter go unsettled." James looked troubled.

"He is a hard revengeful man," Kate said. "What will he do to us?"

"I have heard talk that what has been happening in Rogart might happen in Culmailie," James said uneasily.

"You mean that the Countess might take our land from us, and rent it to a sheep farmer from the south?" Kate looked startled.

"Aye, wife, it could happen. It doesna pay her ladyship to be renting the land in small crofts like ours when she can get more money for it in sheep."

"But there are the hillsides for the sheep. Why should she take our valley?"

"For a sheep-fold. The sheep farmers must have the valleys to winter the sheep."

"Do you mean she might take our fields from us, *our* fields where you have laboured and ploughed and planted, you and your father before you, aye, and his father before him, for many a generation?"

"Aye, just that, wife."

"But there have always been Murrays at Culmailie."

"Soon there may no longer be Murrays here."

"But the house? What will they do with the house? Surely they will not take the very roof from over our heads?"

"What will be the good of a house if there are no fields to till, and no place for the cows to graze?" James asked. "You know what has been happening in other parts of her ladyship's lands where the crofters have had to make way for the sheep."

"They have burned the houses, so the crofters cannot go back to them," she said in a whisper. "But surely that cannot happen to us, James, not to us?"

"It might. The factor is no friend to us and he'll take pay for Davie standing up to him today."

"I wish Davie had never seen that partan!" she exclaimed, almost in tears.

"The trouble would come, partan or no partan," her husband told her. "The partan may only have hastened it. We must wait and see what is to come."

They did not have long to wait.

About a week later Davie and Kirsty were bringing the cows down from the pasture to be milked. Kirsty sang as they followed the beasts, her voice caroling over the hillside. Suddenly her song broke off abruptly. "Look!" she called to Davie. "There's a man standing at our door. There's no one in the house. Mother has gone to sit with old Elspeth Ross, and Father is away to the market at Dornoch."

Davie shaded his eyes with his hand. "The man looks like Adam Young, the factor's man. What does he want of us? It is not the time for the rent to be paid."

"He is nailing a paper to the door!" Kirsty exclaimed. The blows from the hammer echoed up the hillside.

"Hurry, Kirsty!" Davie broke into a run. They left the cattle to meander down the hill-path after them. "Hi!" Davie cried as they approached the house. "Hi, Mr. Young! My father is not home. What do you want?"

The factor's man vouchsafed no reply, but gave a final ding with his hammer to the nail fastening the paper to the door. He was mounting his horse when Davie ran up breathless.

"What's that paper, Mr. Young?"

Adam Young gave a scornful laugh. "Your father will see fast enough. Maybe it'll be a lesson to him not to allow his children to be so impudent to their betters in the future." He gave Davie a prod with the butt-end of his riding whip and cantered away along the grassy road. Davie stared after him, but Kirsty was already at the door.

"What does the writing on the paper say, Davie? You are a better reader than I am."

James Murray had taught both his children to read and to write, and Davie had proved an apt scholar.

"Notice of termination of tenancy," he read out slowly.

"What does that mean?" Kirsty demanded.

"I am not sure. Father is the tenant of this croft. Perhaps it has something to do with that. Yes, it must be, for here is the Countess of Sutherland's name and she owns our land, and here below is Father's name." Davie scanned the paper rapidly. "It is signed by Patrick Sellar."

"That man!"

"There are so many big words, I think it is a lawyer's paper," Davie went on, reading aloud and stumbling among the legal terms, "—hereby give you notice to quit this house and the lands apper—appertaining, by the eleventh of May of the year 1812."

"1812? Why, that's this year, and it's May next month," Kirsty chattered. "Why, what's the matter, Davie?"

Davie had come to an abrupt stop and turned quite pale. "Kirsty, it's a notice to quit that the factor has served on us!"

"To quit? What does that mean?"

"To leave. To give up this house and to go away."

"Go away? From Culmailie?" Kirsty sounded incredulous. "This is our home. You must be wrong, Davie."

"I'm not wrong," Davie said, reading the notice a second time. "Oh, Kirsty, it means we'll all have to get out of here quite soon."

Kirsty looked bewildered. "But where will we go?"

Davie shook his head. "Maybe my father will find another croft."

Kirsty was troubled. "Davie, do you think this has happened because you threw the partan at the factor and I bit him?"

"It could be, Kirsty, it could be." Davie looked worried too.

"Then maybe—maybe—" Kirsty faltered, "if we went to the factor and said we were sorry, he'd take this paper back again and we could still bide at Culmailie?"

"But I'm *not* sorry," Davie said obstinately. "We were in the right about the partan."

"Och, Davie, you're awful dour!" Kirsty bit her lip. "Will you not even say you are sorry to get us to stay?"

"Not even to get the factor to take the paper back and let us bide here will I crawl to him!"

Kirsty was on the verge of tears. "And will you let your pride come before us being turned out of our home? Then I will have to go to the factor and speak to him by myself."

Davie hesitated and Kirsty was quick to see it. "I did not think you would let me face yon awful man alone," she went on.

"No, I will not do that. I will go with you to the factor and ask him to take back the paper, but I will not say I was wrong over the matter of the crab."

"Where shall we find the factor?"

"I am not sure. Maybe we should go to Dunrobin Castle where the Countess lives and ask for him there."

"I—I'd be frightened to go there. Besides, it's nigh on four miles away."

"What are four miles?" Davie said with the contempt of the Highland lad who runs the hills.

"Eight miles altogether, there and back!" Kirsty reminded him.

"If you cannot walk eight miles, then you stay here."

"No, no, I'll go with you," Kirsty said hastily.

"Then let's be on our way before Father comes from the market and sees this." Davie ripped the paper from the nail.

"Wait! First we must milk the cows or they'll be bellowing fit to wake the dead," Kirsty said practically.

When the cows were milked, Kirsty handed him a piece of bread and cheese. "Here, eat this, then go and wash your hands and face."

Davie opened his eyes wide. "Wash myself? For what? It is not the Countess we are going to see, but just the factor."

"All the same, we will go clean and not disgrace our mother," Kirsty replied firmly, and though he grumbled, Davie went out to the well and fetched up a bucket of water to wash himself.

With scrubbed and shining faces they set off along the road to Dunrobin Castle. Under the tartan homespun shawl that was her Sabbath wear Kirsty carried something carefully.

"What have you got there?" Davie asked.

"Our shoes," Kirsty said, revealing them. "Here! You can carry your own now."

"Our shoes!" Davie stopped dead. "What in the name of goodness made you bring those?"

The children only wore shoes on the Sabbath when they went to church. Even then they walked the mile or so barefoot to save the leather, and only put on the shoes when they came within sight of the church.

"We will show the factor that the Murrays are not tinkers, that we have shoes like the best in the land," Kirsty said with dignity. "There will be no call for him then to look with scorn at our dusty feet."

Davie took his shoes from her without a word and tucked them under his arm. They plodded on silently for a mile or two, then Kirsty asked, "What will you say to the factor when you speak with him?"

"I shall ask him to take back this paper and to leave my father and mother to live in peace," Davie told her.

"Will you speak so boldly as that to him?" Kirsty asked, admiring, but slightly alarmed. "Will you not go more softly about it, for, after all, he is the factor?"

"I shall speak plainly, but I will be respectful," Davie decided, and Kirsty had to be content with that.

They passed through the gates of the estate and soon afterwards they came within sight of the great castle of Dunrobin; then with one accord they stopped and put on their shoes. Kirsty drew her shawl more tightly about her. The long avenue with the drifts of last year's beech leaves stretched before them. All was silent except for the light wind that rustled the trees overhead. Kirsty stopped suddenly. "I dare not go to that big door and ask for Mr. Sellar. Oh, Davie, it's frightened I am!"

Davie, too, was a little overawed by the castle, but he was not going to show it. "Oh, dinna be a feartie," he said. "I've been here before with my father to bring a young pig for the Countess's dinner."

"Did she eat a whole pig?" Kirsty's eyes opened wide.

"Och, it's foolish you are! It was for a grand party she was having with a large company. I mind that then my father and I went round to the back of the castle where the servants live. That is what we will do now, and ask there for Mr. Sellar."

They went by a path through some kitchen gardens, then passed the stables, set well apart from the house. There a stable lad, grooming a horse, called to ask them where they were going.

"We are seeking Mr. Patrick Sellar," Davie said with dignity. "Will we be finding him at the castle?"

"Aye, he's there speaking with her ladyship now. This is his horse that I'm grooming."

The lad seemed friendly. Davie was encouraged to ask his advice. "How could I get word to Mr. Sellar? I must speak with him this day."

The stable lad looked at him curiously for a moment. "He is not likely to leave her ladyship to come and speak with you. You would do better to wait for him here. He may be some time, but you will be sure to see him, for he cannot go away without his horse."

Kirsty looked troubled. "Oh dear! We must be home before the night falls."

"James Murray's bairns from Culmailie, are you?"

"Aye," Davie nodded.

"I ken your father. Come into the stable, bairns. You can sit on the hay there and rest."

"But what if Mr. Sellar comes out? We must not miss him."

"You cannot miss him. He will send for his horse to be brought round to the front of the castle, and I will call you then."

It was warm and comfortable in the stable and the children settled down to rest, Kirsty leaning wearily against Davie. Soon her eyes began to blink and before long she was fast asleep. Davie remained awake, staring through the open door towards the castle, waiting, waiting. The sunset tinted the topmost branches of the trees a rosy red, then the sky paled; colour drained from it and the greyness of evening spread about. Davie shifted uneasily. Already they would have been missed at the croft and even now his father might be searching for them. After coming so far, though, it would never do to go back without seeing the factor.

Kirsty stirred, rubbed her eyes and looked about her. Recollection came flooding back. "Oh, Davie, it's getting dark and we're still here! Surely the factor must have gone?"

"Not yet!" Just then there was a clatter of feet across the cobbled yard, and Calum Ross the stable lad came running.

"I've to saddle Mr. Sellar's horse now and lead him round to the foot of the steps below the main door."

"I'll help you with the saddling," Davie offered.

That done, Calum led the horse round the side of the castle, and the children followed him closely.

Mr. Sellar came out and began to descend the steps.

Davie stepped forward between Mr. Sellar and his horse. "Please, sir, may I have a word with you?" he asked respectfully.

Sellar peered at him in the gathering dusk. "You, is it? Murray's lad? Ah, so your sister of the sharp teeth is with you too? Weel, has your father sent you snivelling to ask my pardon?"

"He has not!" Davie cried indignantly. "It is about this paper that we found nailed to our door that we have come."

"Ah! I thought that would sting James Murray," Sellar said with satisfaction. "A crafty piece of work to send his bairns to ask for mercy!"

"He has *not* sent us!" Davie shouted, his temper rising. "My father does not know about this paper. We plucked it down before he saw it."

"That's true, sir," Kirsty added her word. "We came ourselves to ask you to take it back, and—and—to leave us all in peace." She had remembered Davie's words and said them for him.

"You had better take that paper back to your father," Sellar said coldly. "If you do not, you will find yourselves in trouble for interfering with the law." He made a move towards his horse.

"Please, sir, listen to me." Davie stood deliberately in his path. "My father has been a good tenant, always ready with his rent. It—it would break my mother's heart to leave Culmailie—"

"Out of my way, scum! Get back to your pigsty!" Sellar thrust him so roughly aside that Davie stumbled and fell to his knees. Before he could pick himself up, Sellar had his foot in the stirrup and mounted his horse. Kirsty had to jump aside so that she was not under the horse's hoofs as Sellar turned.

Davie flung an arm round her. "You are a wicked evil man, Mr. Sellar!" he called after the factor.

"Steady, lad, it is a chancy thing to be calling the factor names," Calum Ross said. "All the same, he might have taken the time to listen to you."

"All that waiting and we have done no good!" Kirsty burst into tears. "Now it is late and our father will be angry and I am so tired."

"We were better not to have come at all," Davie said with regret. "Come, Kirsty lass, we'll get back to Culmailie." He thrust the paper he held into his pocket and gave a hand to Kirsty.

"First we must take off our shoes," Kirsty said, always the practical one. She slipped off her shoes and tucked them under her shawl. "Let us get clear of all these trees before the night falls." She glanced timidly about her.

"The moon will be rising soon," Davie said reassuringly.

They hurried through the castle lands till they reached the high-road again. They turned left and followed it till they trudged over the bridge that crossed the Golspie Burn and into the village of Golspie. A light shone from the minister's manse and from the school-master's house but most of the windows were already dark, for it cost money to burn candles.

The children were half way through the village when they heard footsteps and saw coming towards them a shadowy figure carrying a lantern. Kirsty clutched Davie. "Oh, is it a robber, Davie?"

"Silly, would a robber be carrying a lantern?" The figure broke into a run towards them.

"It's Father!" Davie exclaimed. "It's Father with the lantern."

"Father! Father!" Kirsty cried, throwing herself upon him. "Oh, Father, it's glad I am to see you!" She burst into tears of relief.

"Where have you children been?" James Murray demanded sternly.

"To Dunrobin Castle. We went to speak with the factor," Davie told him.

"To speak to Mr. Sellar? Why?"

"Because of this paper we found pinned to the door." Davie handed the paper to his father, who scrutinized it by the light of the lantern. His face set in hard lines.

"We thought if we spoke to the factor and I said I was sorry for biting him, he might take the paper back," Kirsty explained. "But he wouldn't listen to us though we had waited such a long time, and and—I'm so tired—" The tears began to flow again. James Murray folded the paper away in his pocket, then lifted Kirsty on to his shoulder.

"Come then, my wee lassie! We'll talk no more about this till we get home. You take the lantern, Davie."

When they reached Culmailie, their mother was at the door watching anxiously. "Is it you, James?" she called out.

"Aye, lass, I've got the bairns safe and sound."

"Thank God for that!" she cried with all her heart.

Soon they were seated by the fire, each with a cup of warm milk and bread and cheese, and while they ate, they told their parents of all that had happened at Dunrobin.

"Is it true what Davie says, that we'll have to leave Culmailie?" Kirsty asked her father.

"Aye, he read the paper right," James Murray said grimly.

"Is it—is it because Davie stood up to him about the partan and—and I bit him?" Kirsty asked.

"No, my lassie, it would have come anyway, though that business may have hastened it. What will happen to us has already happened to many a crofter in Sutherland, and more of us yet will have to go."

"But why must we be turned out of our house?" Davie demanded vehemently.

"To make way for sheep, my laddie. Her ladyship at

Dunrobin can make more money by letting her land to sheep farmers."

"But she is already rich. She dresses in silks and she eats meat three times a day, someone told me."

"No matter! Sheep count for more than men in these days."

Kate Murray had been listening quietly, her face pinched by unhappiness. "For generations the Murrays have lived at Culmailie," she said. "It is out of the memory of man when Culmailie was not farmed by a Murray. Here you were born, James, and to Culmailie I came as a bride, and here your children were born. And now there will be no more Murrays at Culmailie." She bowed her head and they were all silent for a few minutes, then she spoke again. "How long have we, James, before we must go?"

"Five weeks," he said unhappily.

"But where shall we go? Where shall we go?" Kirsty cried desperately. Her mother smoothed her hair.

"Do not weep, my bairn. There will be a way found for us," she said with simple faith, as though, for a moment, the curtain which hid the future had been lifted for her.

2. THE BURNING OF CULMAILIE

For the next few weeks the children seemed to lead much their usual life; herding and milking the cows and feeding the hens. Their mother continued to make butter and cheese and 'crowdie', the soft cheesy curds that David liked so much, but James Murray no longer worked in his fields. He was frequently away at the market at Dornoch, and when he came back there was always one animal fewer in the byre. Then came the day when he sold the pig.

"Did you get a good price for him?" Kate asked anxiously.

"Fair enough, considering there were others with pigs to sell." James handed the money over to her and she put it in the chest which stood beside their bed.

"There will soon be enough," she said, when she rose from her knees beside it.

"Enough for what, Mother?" Kirsty asked.

"Enough for the journey we shall have to take."

"We shall not go till we are forced," James Murray burst out fiercely. "Factor Sellar shall not turn me out of my house easily."

"Oh, James, you will not do him violence? You must not lift your hand to him or he will have you in prison. He is only waiting for that excuse," Kate warned her husband.

"I shall do nothing foolish," James promised her.

The time drew near when the notice to quit the croft would expire. Then, on the 10th of May, the day before they were due to leave, James Murray's brother John arrived on his horse from Dornoch. He wore a troubled face.

"James, can you come at once to Dornoch? Our mother is very ill and the doctor thinks the end cannot be far."

James Murray's mother kept house for John, a bachelor.

John was a carpenter and joiner, employed by many of the owners of big houses in Sutherland.

James looked at his brother in dismay. "Och, John, this is bad news indeed, and it comes at a bad time for us. You know that tomorrow I have to clear out of this house?"

John looked helplessly at his brother. "What will you do, then? Mother is asking for you all the time. Must I go back and tell her you cannot come?"

James made up his mind quickly. "No, you shall not do that. She has been a good mother to us."

"If she is wanting you, then you *must* go," Kate said at once.

"But what will you do about this house when Mr. Sellar comes tomorrow to turn you out of it?" John asked.

"I will write him a letter telling him of my mother's illness and asking him to give us a few days longer. Surely, in the name of mercy he will do that, for the Murrays have been tenants of the Sutherlands for generations."

"Aye, surely, surely! A week cannot make much difference to him."

"I will tell him that if he will grant me this favour for my mother's sake, I will go out quietly when the time comes. Though it goes ill with me, John, to give up this house tamely."

"Aye, it is a sad thing that is happening to folk hereabout. Every market day in Dornoch there are fewer folk there. There's a many have gone across the sea to America."

"Things have come to a pass indeed when the Countess of Sutherland thinks more of sheep on her hills than of men," James said bitterly. "But Kate will give you a bite to eat while I write my letter. Davie, will you saddle the horse for me?"

James took inkhorn and quill and paper from a cupboard. When he had finished writing the letter, he handed it to John to read.

28

"Aye, that's respectful enough and states your case clearly," his brother said. "The factor will be a hard man if he does not grant your request, James."

Davie came in to say the horse was ready. James folded the letter.

"I would send it to Patrick Sellar at Dunrobin, but it might be lost or delayed if it passes through too many hands. Instead I will trust it to you, Davie. Be watching for the factor early to-morrow morning, and give him the letter as soon as he reaches the door."

"I will do that, Father."

"Be mannerly and respectful," his father told him. "I know you have a high temper, but keep it in check. Remember, when I am not here, you stand in my place. Look after your mother and sister. See no harm comes to them."

James Murray went out to mount his horse and the children and Kate followed him to the door.

"I shall be back, Kate, as soon as may be," James called as he rode away.

That night, as Kate and the children ate their simple supper of oatcake and cheese, Davie stared into the glowing embers of the peat fire, thinking of the next day.

"Mother, is the money quite safe that my father got for the cows and the pig?" he asked suddenly.

"It lies at the bottom of the kist." She pointed to the plain oak chest that held her linen and blankets.

"Will it be safe there?" Davie asked anxiously.

"Why, laddie? Why should it not be safe?"

"There will be rough men come with Mr. Sellar to put us out of the house. If they carry out the furniture, who is to say whether they will put their hands inside the kist or no?"

Kate stared at her son. "But the letter from your father? —that will make everything all right. When Mr. Sellar

reads it, then they will go away without touching the furniture."

"It is that I do not trust Mr. Sellar!" the boy blurted
out. "It would be better for the money to be hidden safely
outside the house."

"Where would you hide it, then?" Kate Murray looked
only half-convinced.

"There is a flat stone in the burn. We could put the bag
of money under that. No one would look for it there. I
think my father would have thought it was a wise thing to
do."

Kate rose and went to the chest and lifted out the sheep-
skin bag. "We will put it where you say, Davie, but we
will all go to see where it lies, so we cannot be mistaken
when we go to get it again."

Davie took the lantern and lighted it from the candle.
Even in the darkness Davie had no trouble in finding the
big flat stone. While Kirsty held the lantern, he heaved it
up and Kate thrust the bag into the hollow beneath it.
Davie let the stone down again and stamped it into place.

"And now we will go to our beds," Kate said. "It will
soon be the morn, and who is to know how soon the factor
will be here. We must be up and ready for him."

Davie lay for a time that night with his eyes staring into
the darkness. A strange shiver of foreboding tingled down
his spine. He thought with relief of the money safely beneath
the stone, and then, with the ease of childhood, he fell
asleep. He was wakened by his mother shaking his
shoulder.

"Come, Davie! Get you up! The light is growing over
the treetops in the Balblair Woods. Your breakfast is
ready."

She set the bowls of porridge and the pitcher of milk on
the table. They ate in silence, having no heart to talk, thinking of their father in Dornoch, and of what might be com-

ing to them. When they had finished, Kate washed and stacked the bowls. "Now we will wait and see what happens," she said, standing at the door and shading her eyes as she looked down the hillside towards the road from Golspie.

They had not long to wait. Round the Drummuie Wood came a small procession on horseback, headed by Patrick Sellar. After them rumbled two carts from the estate of Dunrobin carrying axes and sledge hammers.

"Here they come!" Davie exclaimed tensely.

"Why are they bringing hammers and axes?" Kirsty asked.

Davie scowled, but said nothing. At the market in Dornoch he had heard ugly stories of what happened to the houses of tenants who were thrust from their homes. The determined band rode up to the house.

"Where is James Murray?" Patrick Sellar demanded. Davie stepped forward.

"My grandmother is dying, and my father has had to go to her in Dornoch. He told me to give you this letter."

Sellar snatched the letter from him and scowled as he read the contents. "A likely story!" he snorted. "This is only a fine trick to delay matters." He flung the letter to the ground.

"Indeed, sir, it's true, it's true!" Kate cried. "My husband's brother came to fetch him to Dornoch last night. His mother is at death's door. Will you not give us a few days longer to bide here till he returns? It cannot be long."

"Not another day! Not another hour! Get your furniture out of there!"

Kate Murray reeled back as though he had struck her. Davie flushed with anger. He bit his lips to keep back the words.

"Nay, nay, sir!" his mother cried to Sellar. "How can you expect a poor weak woman with two weans to carry out heavy loads? Give us but time, and I will get word to my husband in Dornoch."

"James Murray has had all the past two months to remove his furniture. He should have done it then. No more time at all shall he have! Well, are you going to lift out your wretched possessions?"

"This is our house, that Murrays built long ago with their own hands. They shaped the roof timber and set it in its place and with their own hands they laid the thatch. Think you we shall tamely give it up to you, factor? It is not yours to take!" Kate turned abruptly into the house, and Davie and Kirsty followed her; but instead of making any effort to remove the furniture, she sat down in a chair and motioned Davie to occupy his father's chair on the other side of the hearth, and Kirsty to take the stool at her feet.

The factor's face grew dark with anger. "Into the house with you, men, and bring out all their things! There is no need to be overcareful how you handle them. They are not worth much, and if James Murray wished them to be treated tenderly, he should have seen to them himself."

The men needed no second bidding. They plunged into the house and flung cupboard and table and beds through the door. Davie sprang to his feet.

"You will be sorry for this!" he shouted, but Sellar gave him a cuff across the mouth.

"No impudence from you, you brat!"

A crash drowned Davie's reply. Kirsty wailed, "Oh, Mother! The wedding china *your* mother gave you!"

The wedding china had been cherished and handed down from generation to generation, only used on special occasions. Some day it would have been Kirsty's. Her mother went white to her lips, but she still sat defiantly in her chair. Next the linen chest was flung out and the lid sprang open and the contents were trampled into the mud of the farmyard. Kirsty could stand it no longer. She rushed from the house and gathered up the bed-covers and blankets and the one fine white linen table-cloth that Kate had woven herself when she was a lass. Still Kate said nothing, looking with terrible eyes at the factor who stood watching in the doorway. Under those unflinching eyes he grew uncomfortable.

"There is no need to be over-rough," he said to his men. "Now, Mistress Murray, if you and your son will rise from your chairs, they shall be carried out with care."

"Then you must carry us out with them too, for go from this house on my own legs I will not!" Kate Murray said with determined dignity.

"Remove them!" Patrick Sellar ordered.

The men seized Davie and carried him kicking and struggling from the house. When he would have rushed back into the house, one of them gave him a push which sent him sprawling flat on his face on the trampled ground. They turned their attention to Kate Murray. She rose proudly to her feet.

"The first one of you to lay a finger on me will feel my nails on his face!" she said. Before her the men fell back muttering. No one wanted to be the first.

"We've had enough of this defiance!" Sellar shouted, his temper rising. "Light a torch at the embers of that fire and set it to the thatch! If she will not come out, let her roast alive!"

One of the men snatched up a torch of resin and pine they had brought with them for the purpose of firing the house, and thrust it among the glowing peat. It burst at once into flame. He snatched it out, jumped on the remaining chair and thrust the torch in among the timbers and the thatch. It went up like a bonfire. With the smoke eddying round them the men rushed from the house. Still Kate Murray stood as if turned to stone. Suddenly Davie realised

his mother's peril, and he rushed in and tugged at her arm.

"Come out, Mother! It will only be minutes before the roof falls about our heads!"

Still she stared about her as though bereft of understanding. Davie plucked at her hand. "Mother! Mother! Come out! If you do not, we shall both die here!"

It was only the realisation of Davie's peril that brought her to her senses. As the smoke swirled about them and bits of burning thatch fell at their feet, she ran from the house with him.

"I thought that would smoke out the vixen and her cub!" Sellar mocked.

Kate Murray drew herself up to her full height and she was a tall woman. "A vixen, am I, Patrick Sellar?" she be-

gan pointing her finger at him. "Then hear what a vixen
has to say to you this day!" Her voice sounded so terrible
that all the men fell silent.

"To-day you have shown no mercy to the suffering. Look
then for a day when suffering will visit your own house and
there will be no mercy for you. You have laid your hands
on those who were defenceless, but your time will come
when there will be none to stand beside you when you are
in need. You have put fire to this house, but that fire and
smoke rises to heaven to cry for your punishment. Never will
you go easily again! Never will you be free of the evil you
have done! It will be remembered long after you are dust
in the grave!" A gust of wind sent the smoke eddying round
her in ghostly fashion. Patrick Sellar turned pale and

stepped backward away from her, then made an effort to recover himself.

"You—you dark witch!" he cried. "Don't you dare lay curses on me or I will have you whipped for it!"

She fixed him again with her dark glittering eyes, and his gaze fell. "Have you not brought enough destruction on this house?" she asked him fearlessly. "Go on your way! You have done that for which you came." She turned her back on him with contempt. For a moment he seemed about to reply angrily, then he flung himself on his horse.

"Gather up your gear, men, and come after me," he shouted over his shoulder.

Kate Murray and her children stood watching the men as they clattered away down the hill. Behind them the smoke from the burning thatch was swept across the country by the wind from the sea. Again and again came the crash of the timbers as the roof rafters fell into the house and a shower of sparks shot up. Suddenly, as though her legs would support her no longer, Kate Murray sank to the ground, keening softly to herself. "My bairns! My bairns! What will your father say to this? What a home-coming for him!"

Kirsty burst into tears, but Davie stood manfully, his chin upthrust his legs firmly braced, his whole body expressing defiance and resolution. "Do not weep, mother! We will build a new house, you will see."

"But where, Davie, where?" his mother asked in despair. "The factor would just pull it down again."

"No, not here!" Davie told her. "There will be a place found for us, Mother, you said so. My father will build another house and I will help him."

Kate Murray looked at the boy. "I believe you will, Davie." A spot of rain fell on her hand. She sprang to her feet. "What shall we do? All our goods lying around and the rain beginning to fall. Where can we find shelter?" She looked wildly at the smoking ruin that had been their home.

Davie was stirred to action. "There is still the cart," he said. "They have not damaged that. If we push it against the wall there, it will make a kind of roof and protect the bedding."

They both helped him to push the cart over to an angle of the wall, so that it formed a roof with the two walls for additional shelter. Under it they placed the mattresses and bedding. Kirsty rescued the meal chest and was glad to find that the good hasp on it had saved the meal from being spilled. Kate collected her pots and pans, such as had not been trodden underfoot by the factor's men.

A clucking sound came from the kailyard. "Listen!" Kirsty said, her finger raised. "That's Snowdrop, the white hen. She always makes a carry-on when she's laid an egg. I'll go see what I can find of the other eggs too."

She came back with three eggs in her apron. "Look what I've found! At least we shall not starve."

"I will light a fire of twigs," Davie said, "Then maybe you could manage to cook the eggs for us, Mother. I—I'm beginning to feel hungry." He looked half-ashamed at this admission, as he cast a glance at the smouldering house.

"Aye, there's fire enough there to last us all our days," his mother sighed, but she set about the work of preparing a meal. It helped her to greater calmness.

"Let us collect what furniture we can into a heap against the wall so it will be sheltered a little and not scattered about the place," Davie suggested to Kirsty. When they had finished the meal was ready and the rain had stopped. They drew chairs round the scrubbed table in the farm-yard. Suddenly Davie said, "I like it, eating under the open sky."

Kate Murray shook her head, but she had to smile at the power of youth to find enjoyment even out of misfortune.

"Aye, fine you like it now while the sun is shining, but

wait till the bitter winds blow and the snow comes like white smoke over the green hills. Then you will want a roof over your head and a warm seat by the fire. Where shall we find that?"

"Think you my father will build this house again?" Davie nodded towards the smoking ruin.

Kate Murray shook her head. "Patrick Sellar would come again and destroy it again as soon as it was built. No, Davie, we must go from here and leave Culmailie for ever."

"Where shall we go?" Kirsty lifted her troubled little face.

"I do not know. Your father has talked of many places, Edinburgh, Dundee, Glasgow. He says there is work for people in the cities."

"What is a city like?" Kirsty wanted to know.

"There are many, many houses."

"More than in Golspie or Dornoch?"

"Oh, yes! Your father has heard tell there are so many streets you could get lost in them."

Davie whistled. There was something new and exciting in the thought of a city. "Will there be rows and rows of crofts?"

Kate shook her head. "No. Your father says many of the houses are built on top of each other, without fields or gardens round them."

Kirsty puckered up her brows. "I wonder if I will like that? When will my father be coming?" she sighed.

"We do not know, lassie." Kate stared down the road too. "It may be to-night, or the next night, or the next—" Her voice trailed away unhappily.

When night fell they huddled under the blankets, the cart giving them shelter. Davie had lighted the lantern and set it beside them. There was still a glow of red from the embers of the burned house.

"Your father aye said a prayer. Think you that you could

38

say a word in his place, Davie? Maybe we could sing a psalm afterwards," Kate said.

"God bless us and keep us this night and always, and bring my father back soon," Davie said simply. Then he lifted his voice and sang, "The Lord's my Shepherd, I'll not want." The others joined in, Kate's voice wavering with grief, and Kirsty's piping treble. The sound of their voices reached James Murray as he rounded the hill on his horse and saw the glowing embers of what had once been his home. For a moment he reined his horse in, shocked with surprise, then he urged him forward up the hill.

"There's Father!" Kirsty cried, as she heard the horse's hoofs. They broke off singing and scrambled from under the cart, Davie waving the lantern.

"Are you safe, Kate? Are you and the bairns safe?" James cried in a frenzy as he flung himself from the horse.

"Aye, James, we're safe and sound, but oh! James, your house is gone!" Kate flew to her husband and broke into a torrent of sobs, grief she had bottled up all day.

"Steady, lass, steady! Here, take the horse, Davie!" James Murray's arms went round his wife.

"Your mother, James? Is she—Is she—?"

"Aye, lass, she's gone. She went peacefully in her sleep, but not before she knew I was there and she spoke to me. I think it was a comfort to her to have me there with John. But to think that all this should happen to you while I was away!" James's face grew dark as he stared at the improvised shelter and the pitiful heap of his household goods. "Did Patrick Sellar do this to my house?"

"Aye, he did! He put fire to the thatch and mocked at us as it burned."

"You gave him my letter, Davie?" Murray asked sharply.

"Aye, Father, he had it as soon as he came, and when he had read it he flung it to the ground."

James Murray clenched his fist and black anger rose in

him. "I will go to Dunrobin and deal with Patrick Sellar!"

Kate held him by the arm. "No, James, stay with us now. If you lay a finger on him, Sellar will have you clapped in gaol. Have we not suffered enough? Must we lose you too?"

"Don't go away, Father! Don't leave us!" Kirsty pleaded.

"What shall I do with the horse? There is no stable for him now," Davie asked.

The practical need for his help put the thought of revenge out of James's mind. Though his home had gone, his family remained, and it was for him to look after them. "Dinna fash yourself, my lass," he said to his wife. "I'll bide here wi' you. Turn the horse loose in the pasture, Davie. He'll take no harm there."

With the help of the lantern, Kate searched among her household crocks and found some oatcake and cheese which she brought to James.

"You'll be hungry after your ride," she said. As James ate, she asked him. "What shall we do? It's plain we canna bide here."

James looked thoughtful for a minute. "To-morrow we will set out on our travels just as soon as we have packed our goods in the cart. We will go first to Dornoch. John will find someone to buy our table and chairs and the cupboards. In his work as a joiner, he knows the people who might buy."

"It hurts me to the heart to part wi' the things I've cared for so long," Kate said, "but we canna carry them wi' us everywhere, and John will get us the best price he can."

"And after Dornoch? Where will we go then, Father?" Davie leaned forward eagerly.

James passed his hand across his eyes. "I have heard tell there is work in Glasgow at the cotton mills there. It is different from the work we have done in Culmailie, but we must be prepared for changes. We have to earn our living."

Davie's eyes began to sparkle. "Glasgow! A great city! How soon shall we start, Father?"

"Eager you are, son!" Kate smiled sadly. "For you it is a new life, and to bairns any change is exciting, but for me I leave a good part of my life behind me here in Culmailie."

"No, no, my lass! There's plenty before us yet. We'll find joy in a new life, you'll see!"

"You are as much of a lad looking for new things as Davie is," his wife chided him with a smile.

"How shall we get to Glasgow?" Kirsty asked.

"I have not thought that out yet. There are ships go down the west coast. Maybe we could get one from Ullapool. I have heard the drovers who come to Dornoch Fair speak of Ullapool, but we should have to make our way through the mountains first."

"Would we have to walk all the way?" Kirsty asked.

"Weel, maybe quite a bit o' it, but you can be having a wee ride on the horse or cart when you are weary."

"Oh, shall we be taking the cart?" Kirsty brightened up at this news.

"Surely! How else do you think we shall carry our blankets and cooking pots? We will start in the morning."

"Then we'd better try to get our sleep now, if we're to be up wi' the sun," Kate counselled.

The next day, as soon as it was light, the family was stirring. Davie quickly built a fire of twigs and pieces of wood from the demolished house, then Kate cooked oatmeal porridge over it for their breakfast. Afterwards, while Kate and Kirsty packed up such household goods as they were taking with them to Glasgow, Davie and his father loaded the cart with the furniture they were to leave at Dornoch. At last all the goods were lashed securely on to the cart, and Davie had brought the sheepskin bag of money dripping from the burn.

"Are you ready, Kate?" James asked his wife quietly.

"Aye, I'm ready, James." She gave a quick look at the blackened walls of what had been her clean bright home, then said with a sigh, "Farewell, Culmailie! We may never see you again."

Kirsty began to weep a little, and Davie put out a hand to comfort her. His eyes looked straight ahead to the road before them. "Do not look back, Kirsty," he whispered. "It is better to look forward. Great things there will be for us yet, you will see!"

3. ADVENTURE ON THE ROAD

O N the way to Dornoch they called at the cottage of a
fisherman who wished to purchase James Murray's
boat for his son. A bargain was struck and another small
sum was added to the sheep-skin bag of silver.

"It is not much," James said to his wife, "but we cannot
take the boat with us, and William Blair has been honest
enough to pay for it when he might easily have taken it for
his own once we were away."

"Shall we have a boat in Glasgow, Father?" Davie asked.
He always loved the evenings spent fishing with his father.

James Murray drew his brows together. "True, there is
a river runs through Glasgow, the river Clyde, but I do not
think it will be possible for us to have a boat on it. There
are far too many people in Glasgow to have boats."

"Are there a hundred people, perhaps?" Kirsty asked.

Her question told James that the children had no idea
of what life in the city would be like. "Not hundreds, but
thousands," he replied.

"Thousands?" Kirsty's eyes grew wide. "How ever shall
we get to know them all?"

"You never will. There are all kinds of people in Glasgow,
some good, some bad. When we get there, we must keep
ourselves to ourselves for a time," his Highland caution
made him say.

At Dornoch they left their furniture with John Murray
to sell it for them.

"Aye, James, I'll do my best for ye," he promised. "I'll
send ye the money for the furniture by the hand o' someone
I can trust, once it's sold."

"Thank you, John. And send us word now and again
what is happening at Dornoch and about the coast, will ye?"

"I'll do that, James. Good luck to ye, lad!"

The brothers parted sorrowfully, then James Murray and his family set out on their way across Scotland. This time there was room for them all to ride on the cart. They took the road that ran alongside Dornoch Firth to Invershin.

Spring was early and warm that year, and the broom and the wild rhododendrons vied with each other in splashes of gleaming yellow and gay purples and crimsons all along the banks of the winding Kyle River. Sometimes Davie and Kirsty got down and ran barefoot over the soft grass of the drove road and played hide and seek among the bushes that bordered the river. Often they ran well ahead of the cart.

"I'll race you to the top of that hill!" Davie challenged Kirsty.

"It's no' fair! You've got a start of me!" she objected.

Laughing and panting, stooping to the steep rise, they made their way up behind the broom bushes to the summit of the hill that overlooked the drove road. Davie reached the top first and looked back along the track they had followed.

"I can see the cart!" he cried to Kirsty, then he stood very still, looking hard. Round the bend behind the cart had come a gipsy family. Two men on ponies rode beside the donkey cart which carried their wives. One man was pointing with his whip at James Murray's cart ahead of them, climbing the road up the hill. They said something quickly to the women, who reined in the donkey and stopped. The two men urged their horses forward along the grassy road. Davie watched them intently.

"What is it, Davie? What are you staring at?" Kirsty asked as she reached his side.

"Those two men! Tinkers they are! Why have they stopped the cart and are going by themselves after my father?"

44

"Oh, Davie, you don't think they mean him any harm?" Kirsty looked apprehensive.

"I don't know, Kirsty. Watch them with me, but keep well out of sight behind the bushes."

"Has Father seen them, do you think?"

Davie shook his head. "He has never looked round, and he would not hear their hoofs on the soft turf above the creaking of our cart—not till they got close to him."

"Look! The men are parting company! One is moving behind the bushes on one side of the road and the other has gone into the wood down by the river," Kirsty exclaimed.

"They're taking cover so as to ride ahead of Father and surprise him at the next bend," Davie guessed in an instant. "Kirsty, they're up to no good!"

"Oh, Davie, what will they do?"

"Steal our bag of money and our goods and take away the horse, maybe."

"What shall we do? What shall we do?"

Davie was frightened too, but he knew the need for quick action. He looked desperately along the road in the direction his father would travel. There was a cloud of dust approaching a ford over the river, a moving, shifting cloud of dust.

"Kirsty, look! There's a drove of cattle coming along the road. There'll be drovers with it, maybe with horses. Run as fast as you can across the hill to them and ask them to come and help my father."

"What will you do?"

"Go fight beside him, of course! Run, Kirsty!"

Kirsty needed no second bidding. Soon she was coursing down the hill like a young hare towards the dusty cloud.

Davie slithered down the hill in the opposite direction, running fast where the bushes gave him enough cover, sinking on his hands and knees where the bushes were not high enough to conceal him. He kept an eye on the two tinkers. They were a quarter of a mile ahead of his father now, waiting behind trees where the road took a bend at the foot of the hill. Davie plunged downward to the point of meeting.

The cart rattled on. As it rounded the bend, the two horsemen converged on James Murray.

"Stop your cart!"

James drew rein and looked from one to the other of them. "What do you want?" he asked sharply.

One man drew a thick stick from under his coat, while the other flicked his whip ominously. Kate Murray uttered a startled cry.

"Do as you are told and we will do you no hurt," the man with the bludgeon said. "Have you got money?"

"If I had I would not give it to you," James said defiantly, gathering up his reins and beginning to urge on his horse. The whip lash curled round his wrist, forcing him to drop the rein.

"I can do better than that," the man with the whip jeered at him. "Next time it will be your face. Watch out for your eyes!"

"Now will you give up your money and the horse and your gear?" the man with the bludgeon asked. "We will leave you the cart and maybe a couple of blankets if you will give us no trouble."

James hesitated, loathe to give up his possessions tamely, but knowing he was no match for two men. Kate cried, "Take what you will off the cart, but let my man alone!"

"The money first! I know you crofters. You'll have money with you from selling your goods. You always have!" the gipsy with the stick mocked them.

Still James made no move to give up his possessions. The elder man moved towards him on his horse. "Out with the bag now, or do we have to search you? We shall not be tender with you," he threatened.

Davie had reached a bush some twenty yards away. He felt in his pocket and drew out his catapult made of a

forked twig and a piece of sheep gut. He placed a stone in
the catapult and took aim. The man with the whip raised
it threateningly. Davie let fly. He had no time to take aim
accurately; instead of hitting the man as he intended, the
stone caught the horse on the shoulder. The startled animal
reared high, pawing the air. The gipsy was caught off
balance and flung from the saddle. The whip went spinning
into the bushes as he fell on the road. His horse whinnied
and galloped away as if the devil were pursuing him. This
left only the man with the cudgel, and he, amazed at his
accomplice's mishap, had his attention distracted for a
moment. This gave Davie the chance he needed to take
more careful aim. He bent back the twig ready. The second
gipsy lifted his stick, meaning to bring it down on James
Murray's head. Straight as an arrow the stone sped this
time and hit the man's wrist a sickening crack. He yelled
with pain and dropped the cudgel. Davie could not restrain
a shout of triumph. "Hold on, Father! I'm with you!"

The first gipsy had staggered to his feet again. He snatched up the whip and went tearing among the bushes in Davie's direction, brandishing the whip. Davie, quick as a hare, bent and doubled among the bushes, trying to avoid the wicked curling lash.

James jumped from the cart and pounced on the cudgel the second gipsy had dropped. The gipsy tried to make his horse rear to trample on James, but it was plain from the way he handled the bridle that his wrist was broken. He kicked out at James and yelled to the other gipsy, "Come here with that whip, Matt! It's the man we want! He's got the money!"

Only once did Matt strike at James with the whip, however. Frightened though she was, Kate was not going to stand by doing nothing while her husband and son were attacked.

"A weapon? Where's a weapon?" she cried, searching feverishly among the goods in the cart. The iron saucepan in which she had cooked the morning's hurried breakfast came to her hand, still half full of porridge. She stood up in the cart and brought the saucepan down on Matt's head with all the force she could wield. It cracked down upon his skull, stunning him, and the porridge streamed out over Matt's head and eyes.

"Well done, Mother!" Davie yelled. Kate leaped from the cart and snatched up the whip.

"Now you shall have a taste of your own medicine!" she cried, and ran at the man still sitting on the horse and lashed at him. One blow of the whip was sufficient. The second gipsy dug his spurs into his horse and shot off down the road. James ran to Davie, who was struggling with the fighting, kicking man on the ground.

In the excitement none of them heard the thud of hoofs coming along the drove road from the opposite direction. Two men galloped up, one of them with Kirsty clinging to him, her arms round his waist. They reined in sharply.

"What's going on here?" the elder man cried. James spun round, still keeping his grip on Matt the gipsy.

"Oh, it's you, Donald Rae!" he cried in relief at the sight of the drover, whom he knew well. "We've been set upon by a couple of tinker vagabonds. Here's one of the rascals!"

Donald Rae laughed out loud at the sight of Kate Murray with the whip in her hand, and the gipsy cowering before her on the ground.

"Your wee lassie here said ye were in desperate need o' help, but it seems to me ye've no' been managing badly on your ain. Where's the other rascal?"

James pointed away down the road where the second gipsy was urging his horse along as fast as it would go. Donald chuckled again and peered at the recumbent form of Matt. He got down from his horse and lifted Kirsty down too.

"Let's take a look at this fellow." He stooped over Matt. "Guid sakes, man! Ye're crowned wi' porridge!" He grinned at the sight of the porridge pot lying beside Matt on the ground. "Matt McFie! I could scarcely recognise you!"

Matt McFie struggled to his feet, muttering curses under his breath and scraping the porridge from his face.

"Weel, weel!" the old drover exclaimed. "Up to your wicked tricks, are ye? I was hearing there was a warrant out for your arrest up to Ullapool. Highway robbery, is it no'? Ye ken what the penalty is for that?" Donald Rae stroked his throat meaningly. Matt McFie went pale. He well knew that death by hanging was the judgement on a convicted highway robber.

"Aye, ye'd be weel advised no' to go to Ullapool," Donald Rae told him. "Maybe, though, I should tak' ye wi' me to the cattle fair at the Muir of Ord. I could hand ye over to the justices there, for this time ye've been caught i' the very act."

Suddenly McFie twisted round like an eel and escaped from James Murray's hands. He went away leaping like a roe-deer over the low bushes and growing heather, streaking after the other gipsy on his horse, shouting, "Wait for me! Wait for me!" to him. The second man paused, looked round to see if he were being pursued, then reined in his horse. Matt McFie leaped up behind him, clinging to his waist, and then the horse galloped off in the direction of the gipsy women waiting with the donkey and cart.

"Did they steal anything from ye, James?" the old drover asked.

"No, Donald, thanks be that they did not, though had it no' been for Davie here wi' his catapult and Kate wi' her porridge pot, things might no' have gone so weel for us. I was right glad to see you, man."

"It wasna much I did for ye," Donald said. He began to laugh. "I must say, Mistress Murray, ye're a grand hand in a fight! Oh, the way ye wielded yon porridge pot! We were just in time to see it. Wumman, they should enlist ye in the British army to fight the French!"

They all laughed heartily, as much that the strain was over as at the joke.

"Tell me though, James, what ye're doing so far from Golspie and journeying west?"

The two men had often met at cattle fairs in the east and knew each other well. James recounted to Donald how he had been turned out from his croft and the house fired.

"Aye, 'tis happening all up and down the Highlands," Donald commented. "But where are you going with your family, James?"

"To find a ship that will take us to Glasgow. I hear there is plenty work to be had there."

Donald shook his head a little sadly. "True, true! But it is work under a roof from dawn till night, mostly wi' the clatter o' machinery round ye. How will ye like that after the quiet peace o' the hills, man?"

"If there are no crofts for us, then we must do something to earn our bread," James said bitterly.

Just then the cattle came ambling round the bend, cropping the grass of the roadside as they came along.

"We'll have to leave you now, James." Donald Rae shook hands solemnly all round, adding with a twinkle at Kate, "Ye're a bonnie fetcher, mistress, I'd rather have ye on my side than against me."

They parted company with many backward glances and waving of the hands.

That night the Murrays slept in the barn of the inn at Altnacealgach. The next day when they took their leave of the landlord he asked, "Ullapool, is it?"

"Aye, we are looking for a ship to Glasgow."

The landlord shook his head doubtfully. "If ye find no ship," he said, "there is an honest fisherman, Patrick Cameron, who might be able to help ye. Look for him."

The day's journey was uneventful. They saw no more gipsies as they followed the drove road. It led them by a river into which rushing streams poured down from the hills on either side. The path began to mount higher and higher to the gap between the mountains of Cul Mohr and Crioc an Sassunnach. The road grew rough and stony and James Murray had to stop now and again to rest the horse. All around them was the sound of many waters. At last they reached the top of the pass. Davie stood, his hand shading his eyes, peering at the dozen or more lochans that glinted in the sun and the great peaks that swept upward to the sky in the west, and his heart lifted with them.

"Will there be mountains in Glasgow, Father?" he asked.

"I do not think so, Davie. Just streets and houses."

Davie looked puzzled. He could not imagine a land without mountains.

The road began to drop down now towards Strath Kanaird to the coast, then turned along the shores of Loch Broom towards Ullapool. They crossed a little river and immediately came on the town, nestling along the shores of its bay and overhung by the long precipitous face of rock behind it. The smoke went up from over two hundred chimneys. New-looking cottages were grouped round a small harbour, with other small streets behind.

"It is even bigger than Dornoch!" Davie exclaimed.

"Is Glasgow as big as this?" Kirsty asked.

"Bigger, my lassie!"

"Oh!" Kirsty's eyes grew big.

"These look good houses," Kate remarked wistfully, thinking of the destroyed home they had left behind them.

"Aye, they have been built by the British Fishery Society for the fishermen. There's many a barrel of salt herring sent from Ullapool to Glasgow. Now we must ask if there's a ship to take us to Glasgow. Hold the horse, Davie, while I go talk with those fishermen at the quayside."

The men paused in their work of cleaning the nets when James hailed them.

"For Glasgow?" one asked. "That's a thing can only be answered when a ship arrives here, man. In the herring season there are likely to be boats, but no' at this time o' year."

Troubled, James asked, "Is there no regular sailing of a ship from Ullapool to Glasgow?"

The man shook his head. "Whiles a ship will come up the coast bringing sugar and tobacco and the goods they make in Glasgow, but naebody kens when that will be. It might be to-morrow, or a week or a month."

James felt desperate. Had he come all the way across

Scotland only to fritter away his small store of money while they waited for a Glasgow-bound ship? Then he remembered what the inn-keeper had told him. "Is there one among ye named Patrick Cameron?" he asked. "Why, yes? Here I am!" One of the older men in the group looked up quickly.

"The inn-keeper at Altnacealgach told me you might be able to help me to get to Glasgow."

"But I do not take my ship to Glasgow. If it had been Stornoway in the Isle of Lewis, now." The man broke off suddenly. "Why, there is a ship goes every week from Stornoway to Glasgow, taking herring barrels and kelp from the seashore that is used in the chemical works. Maybe, if you could get to Stornoway, you could get a passage in that boat."

"Could you take me to Stornoway with my wife and children?" James asked.

"Well, that I might be doing. To-morrow I go to Stornoway to bring over cattle from Lewis to sell at the cattle fairs at Muir of Ord and Crieff. Could ye help me to sail the boat?"

"I could indeed," James said at once. "I have been used to boats all my life. What would you charge us, now, to take us to Stornoway?"

The fisherman considered. "If you could help me with the boat I would not be needing a man with me, and one of the cattle-men would help me to sail the boat back. How many are there of you?"

"Myself and my wife and two weans."

"Then could you be paying me six shillings, maybe?"

"Yes, I would be willing for that," James agreed.

"To-morrow then, you will be here at the quay at five o'clock in the morning so we can get the tide."

"I will be here, but first I must sell my horse and cart. D'ye ken anyone who would buy them from me?"

Patrick Cameron shook his head. "No. You will have to make enquiries, man."

James returned to his family and told them of the arrangements he had made. "To go to Stornoway seems the best thing to do, but first we must sell our horse and cart. We cannot go till that is done."

"I wonder who might buy our horse and cart?" Kate said.

"I think I know a way to find out," Davie laughed. "Did you no' say you could be doing with some more oatmeal, Mother?"

"Why, yes, I did, Davie."

"Will you spare me some money to go buy some, then? I might hear of someone wanting a horse while I am in the shop."

"I'll come with you, Davie," Kirsty said at once.

"Bless the bairn! He thinks of things!" Kate laughed as the two children rushed away.

"I think I will go down to the harbour and see if I can earn a fish for our supper by helping the fishermen with their nets," James said.

Davie made his purchase at the small shop. It was plain that the old lady who kept the shop was full of Highland curiosity about him, and that prompted her to ask questions.

"Strangers ye are here, surely? Is it far ye've come?"

"From Culmailie."

"Where will that be, now?"

"It is near Dornoch, on the other side of the country."

"I have heard of Dornoch. A long journey ye are from home."

"Aye, but we go a longer journey yet," Davie said. "To-morrow we are going to Stornoway in Patrick Cameron's boat."

The old lady liked to hear news. Her shop was the means of passing on information in Ullapool.

"We are going to find a new home," Kirsty added. "Our own one was burned down."

The shop-keeper leaned across her counter. "How did that come about?"

Davie told her the story. "And now we are going to Glasgow from Stornoway. My father says there will be work for us there."

"To Glasgow! Think of that!"

"Aye, but we cannot go till we have sold our horse and cart," Davie told her, warming to his task. "If you could tell us of anybody needing a horse, I'd be rare obliged to ye, mistress."

"Weel, now, there is the old minister, Mr. McGregor. He has been complaining of the rheumatism in his feet this long time and saying he cannot visit his congregation because of it. He might buy your horse, now, if your father does not place too high a price on him, and the cart too."

"I will tell my father. We are very grateful to you, mistress."

"You can tell the minister that Mistress Robertson at the shop sent you to him." She beamed on both of them.

When they reached the place where they had encamped Davie found that his father had gone down to the harbour. Davie told his mother what he had heard in the shop, and proposed that he should take their horse and cart to show the minister.

"Will it no' wait till your father comes back?"

"Suppose someone else sells the minister a horse before we have shown him ours?"

"It does not sound as though the minister has been in a hurry to buy a horse. Still, there might be no harm in asking him. It will give him time to think about it."

"He has had a lot of time to think about buying a horse already," Davie said shrewdly. "It would be better, perhaps, to take him quickly. What price does my father want for the horse and cart?"

"He wondered if we could get five pounds for it, though we might have to let it go for less to get a quick sale."

Davie caught the horse as he grazed and began to back him between the shafts of the cart. "Will you come with me, Kirsty?" he asked.

In no time at all Davie and Kirsty were jogging along the road to the manse. The minister was rather surprised when Davie was ushered into his study by the small maidservant. Davie had some difficulty in explaining his errand, but at last he made the minister understand.

"Ah, so Mistress Robertson thinks I would be better for having a horse, does she? Ah weel, it's a sensible woman she is! Maybe she is right."

"Will you look at the horse then, sir? I have brought him here for you to see. He stands at your door."

The minister's eyebrows shot up in astonishment. "Young man, you waste no time, but maybe I had better look him over. It would never do to buy a pig in a poke."

"But it is not a pig I am wanting to sell, sir. It is a horse." Davie began to wonder if the minister could be a little deaf.

"Ach, boy, it's speaking in proverbs I am!" the minister chuckled. "Let us be looking at this horse of yours, then."

Kirsty was holding the horse at the gate. The minister walked slowly round the animal, looking at him from all sides.

"He is a good-tempered beast and strong too," Davie said persuasively. "Look, sir, he has good teeth." He pulled open the horse's mouth in the way he had seen the horse dealers do at Dornoch Fair.

The minister seemed amused. "Aye, he seems a good sound horse. It's true I have a stable, but—" He hesitated.

Kirsty looked at the minister. "He has been a good horse

to us. We would like him to have a good home. Will you not buy him, sir? *You* would treat him kindly."

Perhaps that clinched matters for the minister. He patted Kirsty's shining hair. "Weel, ye're a coaxing bit lassie, but maybe what you say weighs with me more than the horse's good teeth. What does your father want for the horse?"

"Five pounds, sir," Davie said promptly, though his natural honesty made him add, "Though he might take less for a quick sale."

"You can tell him to come and see me this evening, then."

Davie looked at him, delighted. "Is it a bargain, sir?"

"Aye, you can call it that."

"Then here's my hand on it," Davie said in his most grown-up style, offering his hand as he had seen the drovers do in the cattle market.

The minister solemnly shook hands with him. "Is it no' the fashion to offer a penny to seal the bargain?" he asked, his eyes twinkling. "Here, then, is the penny, my lad. And here is one for the lassie too. Maybe you will find some sugar-cone at the shop of that excellent woman, Mistress Robertson."

Davie and Kirsty had hardly words to stammer their thanks.

That evening James Murray went to the minister to conclude the deal and returned five pounds better off, and well pleased with the minister's words. "And ye've got a grand straightforward, well-mannered pair o' bairns, James Murray. They do you credit."

That night they packed up their bundles of blankets and household gear that they were taking with them. The children slept well, but their parents little, as they watched for the first blink of dawn. By five o'clock they joined Patrick Cameron at the quayside and handed their bundles aboard. Patrick Cameron steadied the boat and they climbed down the ladder into the ship. Cameron pushed off from the quay and James helped him to hoist the sail. The wind blew off the land and soon they were speeding down Loch Broom and heading out into the wider waters of the Minch.

They came to Stornoway in the late evening and entered the harbour there. It was crowded with fishing craft. After Patrick Cameron had climbed the ladder on to the quay, he surveyed the shipping.

"Ah, there is Peter Mathieson's sloop, the *Catriona*. She will be sailing with the tide to Glasgow with salt herring and kelp. Come with me, James Murray, and I will have a word with Peter and ask him to give you a passage."

Peter Mathieson consented to take them all for a matter of twelve shillings, the Murrays to bring their own food with them.

"Ye can come aboard now. We sail wi' the morning tide. There is only one cabin, but if ye've got blankets, ye'll tak' no harm on the floor."

He helped them to transfer their gear aboard. There was a strong smell of fish, and an even more overpowering smell of sea-weed from the cargo of kelp.

"I hope the smell o' the kelp willna turn ye up," Mathieson said candidly. "It gets higher as we go along, but ye'll just have to thole it. There'll be a thousand worse smells in Glasgow, ye'll find."

Davie and Kirsty wondered what he meant. They were soon to know.

After the ship sailed next morning they knew little but the heaving seas, save for brief glimpses of the mountainous shores as the ship sailed south. Kirsty was sea-sick and lay in the cabin tended by Kate, but Davie scarcely ever left the deck, save to sleep at night. He loved to stand by Peter Mathieson at the wheel and watch him navigate the ship. Now and again Peter let him take the wheel while he stood by. For Davie it was a wonderful beginning to a great new adventure.

4. THE GREAT CITY

THE *Catriona* beat her way up the river Clyde, tacking from side to side of the channel which led to Glasgow's quay at the Broomielaw. Luckily a westerly wind helped to bring the ship along between the narrowing banks, and it was not till she was almost at her destination that she had to be assisted by ropes to warp her in to the quay.

Seasickness forgotten, Kirsty sat at the forepeak of the ship with Davie and watched the changing scene with astonished eyes. They both stared at the long sloping streets with high buildings which ran down from Argyll Street to the Broomielaw, the bridge at Jamaica Street with its seven great arches across the Clyde, and the spire of the Gorbals Church on the horizon behind. Kirsty began to count the church spires, but stopped short when Davie noticed the tall chimneys with the plumes of smoke.

"What are those?" he called to Peter Mathieson.

"Glasgow folk call them stalks. They're high chimneys to carry the smoke of the factories above the houses."

"Factories? What are factories?" Kirsty asked.

"Big buildings where they make goods like cotton cloth. Ye'll no doubt ken about them soon enough," he added grimly.

Davie might have asked him what he meant, but Kirsty was exclaiming at the size of the houses, several storeys high.

"There are houses built on top of houses, as many as five! I would not have thought there were so many houses in the whole world!" A sudden thought struck her. "Where shall *we* live, Mother?"

Kate Murray stared too at the unfamiliar buildings, so different from the low thatched roofs of Sutherland. "Where indeed?" she breathed with a sigh. "Oh, James, I had no idea Glasgow would be so big, with so many people. Where shall *we* find a place?"

James Murray himself was feeling slightly overwhelmed, but he did not show it to Kate and the children. "Ach! In such a big city there's bound to be somewhere for us to stay," he pronounced in greater confidence than he felt.

At last the *Catriona* was brought alongside the quay at the Broomielaw. James, Kate and the two children collected their bundles and said farewell to Peter Mathieson.

"Have ye any idea of a place where we might stay?" James asked him.

Peter shook his head. "I always sleep aboard," he told them. "Ye could ask the minister of the Ingram Street Church. Folk call it the Gaelic Chapel for the Highlanders. The minister is Mr. McLaren. He might be able to advise ye."

"We'll go to him. How do we reach Ingram Street?"

"Go up Jamaica Street there," Peter Mathieson pointed, "then turn right, along Argyll Street and ask again. I'm no' just sure o' the streets masel'."

They shouldered their burdens and set off.

The amount and speed of the traffic in Argyll Street shocked them to bewilderment as they stood on the causeway and watched horses, carts, chaises, coaches, sedan-chairs with runners to carry them, race up and down the street. The shouts of the riders and drivers, the clatter of hoofs on the cobble stones, the crack of whips, sounded deafening to their unaccustomed ears.

"I canna believe it! Where can all these people be hurrying and scurrying?" Kate asked James. "Which way do we go now?"

He shook his head and turned to ask a small poorly-dressed man who was standing idly on the causeway. "Which way do we take to Ingram Street, please?"

The small man looked at them with foxy curiosity. "Ye

cross the road and go up Queen Street there. That'll bring ye to Ingram Street. Strangers here, are ye?"

"We are indeed," James replied.

"Frae the Highlands?"

"Aye, we've just stepped off the boat from Stornoway," James replied with the open innocence of a country man.

The small man eyed them. "Have ye ony place to go?"

James shook his head. "I was going to the minister of the Ingram Street Church to ask his advice."

"I doubt if ye'll find him at his hame the day," the small man said quickly. "This is the day the ministers go out visiting their congregations. But maybe I could put ye i' the way o' finding a place."

"That would be right civil of you, sir," James said gratefully. The sky was overcast and he felt he must find some shelter before the threatened rain soaked them and their blankets and packs.

"It all depends what ye want. Would ye be thinking o' a single end?" the man enquired.

"A single end? What's that?" asked Kate.

"One room, mistress."

She hesitated. "We've always had two rooms before, but maybe we could make-do with one at first."

"Aye, it would give us time to look round and—and get work," James agreed.

"Work's a bit difficult to come by, except for bairns," the man told him, "but maybe ye've got a bit money saved?"

James nodded.

"Aye, weel, then," the small man said briskly, looking rather pleased, "if ye'll mak' do wi' one room, I think I know just the place for ye. It's lucky for ye the wife's father died and was buried twa days syne, and the wife's mother is moving in wi' us. She'd speak to her landlord for ye to have her room," he added glibly.

"Would she, do you think?" James asked.

"Aye, but mind now, it's awfu' difficult to get a room i' Glasgow. There's a wheen folk after places to live in, especially since so many o' the Irish came over to work in the cotton mills. They'll pay onything to get a roof over their heads. Why, I ken one cellar, a *cellar*, mark, now, where there are eight folk living, two to each corner!"

James and Kate looked at each other in consternation. This was not what they had expected of the great city.

"Oh, I wouldna like that! We've always lived decently," Kate exclaimed.

"I'm sure ye have, mistress, I'm sure ye have. That's why I'm telling ye about the wife's mother. A widow woman she is, poor soultie, so ye'd no' be grudging her a wee gift o' money for speaking for ye to the landlord?"

"Weel, no!" James hesitated. "But what kind of a room is it? We wouldna' be wanting to share wi' other folk."

"A pity, that! Ye could do weel wi' a lodger or twa to help pay the rent. The room, now? Weel, it's up a stair at the top o' a house, I'll no' deny, but maist folk like to be at the top o' a stair. There's no' so much noise."

"Is there a window?" Kate asked. She had heard of attics.

"Aye, there's a window, though it's in the roof, ye ken. But I'll tak' ye there. Come on across the road after me."

The man stepped boldly among the traffic and the Murrays plunged after him, though Kate cast frightened glances as they dodged almost under the noses of the horses. They followed the man along the wide street of the Trongate with its high buildings on either side, lined with shops that sold so many strange goods. Kirsty and Kate would have liked to linger to look in the windows, but the man hurried them along. On the other side of the road was the Tron church with its tapering steeple. They came to the arches of the Tontine Hotel with an imposing array of coaches drawn up before it. A little further on the Tolbooth Steeple with its clock and crown towered above them.

The man turned abruptly up a wynd behind the Trongate which led in turn to a narrow close : a shocking change from the spacious Trongate. The buildings on either side were so close that they seemed to lean towards each other, almost touching at the roofs. They made the close like a dark tunnel.

A horrible stench filled the air. It came from a heap in the middle of the close.

"Oh, how it smells!" Kate could not help exclaiming.

"Och, that's naething to worry about, mistress," the small man said lightly. "When the midden gets full the menfolk spade it out into the close and sell it to a farmer for manure. The farmer 'll come soon and cart it awa' to his fields outside Glasgow. Every tenant gets a share o' what the farmer pays, so the midden helps to pay the rent, ye ken. Onyway, ye'll be weel above it at the top o' the house. Up the stairs wi' ye, noo!"

They followed him up three flights of dirty stone stairs with three or four ragged small children sitting on them, till they reached a rickety landing where a door hung crookedly on a latch.

"Here we are!" the man said, opening the door. It gave on to an attic with a cum-ceiled window. Two broken panes of glass were jammed up with rags. There was a tiny rusty fire-place and down its chimney the rain-water was already trickling. Beside it stood a bucket and there was a box-bed built into the corner. On it was a filthy straw mattress bursting its cover. An old woman in a ragged dress and shawl put back a tattered blanket and rose from the bed and peered short-sightedly at them standing in the doorway.

"Weel, Grannie Ferguson!" the small man greeted her.

"Och, it's you, Bob Anderson!" she said with a sniff. "What'll you be wanting?"

"I've brought a man who'd like to rent your room. Ye'll be moving in wi' your daughter, noo your man's deid?"

"My rent's paid to the end o' the week. I canna be turned oot till then," the old lady said in a fighting voice.

"Naebody wants to turn ye oot, Grannie," the man said in a coaxing way. "But supposing ye were to be paid, and paid weel, for letting these folk have your room?

"Weel, noo, that's a different story," she said. A greedy look crossed her face. "How much?" she asked abruptly.

"Ten shillings noo?" the man suggested, looking at James, who could only nod helplessly.

"Ten shillings and my rent's paid to the end o' the week! I'm no' a fool!" The old woman laughed coarsely. "A golden sovereign I'm asking."

"But I cannot be affording that. I'm a poor man. We've just lost our house in the Highlands," James exclaimed. He began to back away.

"Shall we go and look for another place?" Kate asked, wrinkling her nose a little.

Bob Anderson drew the old woman aside and whispered urgently in her ear. "Don't ask too much or you'll lose them. Leave it to me." He returned to the landing where James was consulting with Kate as to whether they should go or not.

"Ye'll no' find it easy to get as good a place as this and all to yourselves, too," he said. "The old woman will tak' fifteen shillings and I'll tak' the other five shillings for my trouble. I was going to ask ten, but seeing ye're strangers and poor Highlanders, I'll be content wi' five. There!"

"Maybe we'd better take it," James Murray said in a low voice to his wife. "It'll give us a roof over our heads while we look for another place." He turned aside and felt in his pocket. Bob Anderson watched him closely, his eyes giving a flicker of greed. James handed the coin to the old woman, who bit it first to make sure it was good.

"Right, Bob Anderson!" she said. "You can carry down the mattress for me and I'll give ye your share o' this when we reach my daughter's house." She held the gold coin between finger and thumb then said, "And this is where I'll keep it for better safety," and she slipped it under her tongue! Bob Anderson picked up the mattress and they descended the stairs, the old lady carrying her blanket in the bucket.

The Murrays stood looking at each other as the sound of the footsteps on the stairs died away.

"Weel, we've got a place of our ain," James said heavily.

"Oh James. I didna think it would be like this in the great city!" Kate began to weep a little. "Oh, how it smells! What I'd give for a breath of our clean Highland air!"

Kirsty began to sniff too. "It's awfu' *dirty*! Oh, Mother! There's an insect crawling up the wall!"

"Losh! The place has got bugs too!" Kate exclaimed.

"Have ye got nothing to grumble at?" James asked his son in desperation.

"Give me some money, Father, and I'll awa' down to the street."

"For what?" asked his mother.

"To buy a bucket and to draw water at the well. We're going to need water. There'll be a well in the street somewhere."

Kate pulled herself together. "Ye're right, Davie. There's no sense in weeping. We've got to *do* something. While ye're in the street buy some soap too. I've got a scrubbing brush somewhere in these bundles. We'll make a start by scrubbing this place out."

"Wait for me, Davie! I'll come with you," Kirsty cried. The two set off down the stair.

Kate and James faced each other. "Dinna be so troubled, Kate," he begged her. "The room'll look better when there's a fire in the grate and we've got some furniture round. When the bairns come back I'll go look for firewood and coals, and see if I can find an old table and chairs and another bed."

"It'll be all right, James. It—it's just the strangeness of everything after Culmailie. We'll get by, you'll see, and we'll make a new life of it, once you've got steady work."

"Aye, I must be looking for something to do. Wi' the bairns here, the place'll soon begin to look like home, and if I get a good job, maybe we'll get two rooms soon."

"Aye, the bairns are a great help," Kate agreed. "Davie's the one for always seeing what's to be done, and Kirsty's no' far behind him."

Little did they know how much they were to rely on their children in the months to come!

Kate worked hard, with Kirsty's help, in getting their room clean, though it meant a lot of journeys up and down the steep stair to fetch water from the well.

Hardly had they got the room habitable than they had a surprise visitor. The door was suddenly flung open and a red-faced burly man confronted them. He was as surprised to see them as they were to see him!

"Where's Grannie Ferguson?" he demanded.

"She'd gone to live with her daughter," James explained. "We've taken over her room from her."

"Oh, ye have, have ye?" the man exclaimed wrathfully. "And without so much as a word to me! What d'ye mean by it?"

James stared at him. "Are ye—are ye the landlord?"

"To be sure I am!"

"Then Mistress Ferguson said she would speak to you for us to have this place."

"She did, did she?" the man looked at James narrowly. "And how much did ye pay her for that service?"

"A—a sovereign!" James faltered. "Did she no' speak wi' ye?"

"She did not! A right bad old woman she is!" The landlord looked about him. "I could put ye out, ye know! Ye seem to have made yourselves at home."

"We—we'd be willing to pay rent," James said.

The landlord's wrath subsided. It sounded as though the Highlander had some money, and that was all that mattered to him.

"Twa shilling the week!" he said promptly, naming a sum twice the amount that Grannie Ferguson had paid. "And if ye can pay that auld witch a sovereign to get into the place, maybe ye'd be willing to pay me, the rightful landlord, the same?"

There was nothing else for James to do, unless he wanted to carry his furniture down all the stairs. Reluctantly he parted with another sovereign and the landlord pocketed it.

"The rent'll be due on Saturday," he announced. "See ye have it ready!" and with that he turned on his heel and stumped down the stairs.

James began at once to look for work, but with the Irish incomers willing to work for very little money, there were far too many men going after far too few jobs. Nobody seemed to have any use for a man who had once been a farmer.

"Why not go and ask Mr. McLaren," Kate suggested. "He's from the Highlands. Maybe he would know of work for you."

Mr. McLaren shook his head sadly when James appealed to him.

"There are many of my congregation who have come down from the Highlands like yourself and cannot find work. If you knew something about machinery, now? Do ye know anything of the new steam-engines that are being used at the cotton factories to drive the spindles and weaving shuttles?"

James shook his head. "I know nothing of engines, though I'd be willing to learn. Is there no work you know of, minister? I'd put my hand to anything. I'm frightened of using up my little store of money and I've a wife and twa children to keep."

"Children, have ye?" the minister asked. "What age are they?"

"Ten, rising eleven."

"Ach, weel, *they* might get work at a cotton-factory. They take bairns there to work with the spinning. They say it's light work, suitable for children. That might be some help."

James looked at the minister earnestly. "It would be a shameful thing, sir, for an able-bodied man to have to depend on his bairns for his keep."

"Doubtless, man, doubtless! But it might tide you over till you find work for yourself. Many Glasgow bairns go to work at *five* years old. You see, the employers would have to pay a lot more for adult labour. Children are cheaper."

"All the same, I'd rather find work myself. If ye hear o' anything, minister, will ye let me know, please?"

"Aye, I'll do that, though I cannot hold out a lot of hope. I'll write your name and address in my book, and I'll visit you when my rounds take me to the Trongate," the minister promised. "But see that you attend the kirk as ye should."

James went back and told his family what the minister had said. To his surprise both Davie and Kirsty wished to go to work in the cotton mills.

"There's nothing for us to do here, Father," Davie said. "No cattle to herd and no crops to look after."

"Not even hens to feed!" Kirsty added disconsolately.

"There's nowhere to go fishing, either!" Davie added. "I fair miss our boat." He sighed.

Kate, too, was not against the idea of the children going to work.

"Ye canna keep children indoors all day," she said, "especially stirring bairns like ours, and I dinna like the notion of them wandering the streets. There's no knowing what accident or wickedness might befall them there. Besides, we've never brought up our children to be idle. They'd be better to learn a useful trade."

With misgivings, James Murray took his children to a cotton mill at Bridgeton. It was a building on two floors with many long windows. From it there came such a clatter of machinery that Kirsty shrank back.

"Whatever's that terrible noise?" she asked.

"Just the machinery, Kirsty, that's all," Davie told her.

"Do we have to work with that horrible din in our ears all the day?"

"We'll get used to it," Davie said lightly, eager to see the new machinery.

The clangour increased as they went up a flight of steps into the mill. As they entered the room a blast of hot dust-laden air rushed out at them and the noise of the machinery almost deafened them. The fine fluff that rose from the machines set Kirsty coughing. Children, thin, pale and tired, stood by the machines, darting at them constantly to do some operation. James Murray felt a pang of misgiving as he looked for the overseer.

A grim-faced man stepped forward. "Weel, what is it? Do ye wish your bairns to be taken on?"

"Yes—" James hesitated. "I—I wondered if you'd got work for me too?"

"No! Only for bairns. What's their age?"

"Ten, rising eleven. They're twins."

"Is their health good? The mill doctor will have to give them a certificate to say they're fit for work."

"They've never had an illness in their lives," James said.

"Right! They can start at once and bring me a line from the doctor before the end of the week. No wages for three days while they're learning, and after that, twa shillings the week, each. That's as good wages as ye'll get anywhere in Glasgow."

"What time do they start in the morning?"

"Six o'clock sharp and no nonsense! Lazy bairns feel the weight o' my hand. An hour off at twelve to eat their dinner and half-an-hour in the afternoon to eat their piece and they finish at half-past seven."

"It's a long time for young children to be standing by their machines." James looked troubled.

"Hoots, man! They soon get used to it. Ye're lucky to get them taken on here, for the boss doesna let bairns do night-work. Other mills do! The sooner they get started, the better. Hi, Maggie!" he called to a child smaller than Kirsty. "You take the lassie and show her how to piece the threads, and Tom, you find this lad a job alongside you."

The children hurried away to the long lines of whirling spindles. The overseer turned to James and took the children's names, then turned away. "Hi, you, Ben Guthrie!" he shouted. "What d'ye think ye're doing, sitting down when my back's turned?"

There was a frightened wail from the luckless Ben as the overseer advanced towards him, arm raised, and there was the sound of a strap descending. James Murray went away with a heavy heart.

Maggie took Kirsty towards the whirring spindles and shouted in her ear above the din of the machines, "Ye watch the bobbins for the thread breaking as it's twisting on the spindle. If it breaks, ye stop the spindles with this lever, then twist the threads together again like this, and then pull the lever and start the machine again. That's all there is to do, but watch ye don't get your hand caught in the machinery."

"What a lot of bobbins to watch!" Kirsty shouted back, bewildered.

"Aye, ye've got to keep on your toes all the time! There's a thread snapped! *You* piece that one together like ye saw me doing."

Kirsty fumbled and managed to twist the two ends together and start the frame spinning again. "Och! It makes me dizzy!" she cried.

"Ye'll get used to it," Maggie told her.

Davie was set to lift the bobbins from the machines as they filled and to set in new bobbins. His was a job of constant watching and fetching and carrying. All the time the overseer kept his eye on the children all over the factory floor, and woe betide any who flagged in their efforts! He kept his strap in his hand, and it came down heavily on their shoulders.

When the whistle blew at twelve o'clock the machinery slowed down to a stand-still and the children, jostling and shouting, poured out of the mill into the yard and found places where they could sit on the hard-trampled ground with their backs to a wall. Many of them wolfed down their 'pieces' as fast as they could and fell asleep as they swallowed the last mouthful.

Davie and Kirsty had brought 'pieces' with them of cheese and oat-cake. They were unlucky in that they had not found places in the sun and the chill wind curled about their shoulders. Kirsty shivered.

"It's awful cold after the heat inside the mill," she said.

"Aren't you going to eat your piece, Kirsty?"

"I—I just couldna, Davie. My mouth feels full o' the fluff from the cotton, and my head aches so with the din o' the machines."

"Och, Kirsty, you must take a mouthful or two. It's a long time to go without food till we get home to-night." Davie looked anxiously at his twin. "Try, now!"

Kirsty took a bite or two, then stopped. "I can't, Davie! It just chokes me. You eat it for me. If—if only I could have a drink—"

Just then Maggie Hunter came along. When she saw Kirsty's white face, she stopped. "Are ye no' weel, my lassie?" she asked.

"She might feel better if she could get a drink," Davie said.

"You her brother? Here, then, take my cup!" Maggie produced a dirty cracked cup from her pocket. "There's a pump near the boiler house if ye can get near to it."

There was a queue of children waiting to draw water, but at last Davie got the cup filled and carefully carried it to Kirsty who drank thirstily.

"Will ye be able to go on with your work, Kirsty?" Davie asked.

"Of course she will! It's the first time that's the worst," Maggie Hunter declared. "It'll no' be as bad to-morrow. Ye can lean up against me, Kirsty, and shut your eyes for a wee while when the overseer's at the other side o' the mill."

Somehow Kirsty managed to struggle through the rest of

that day, though at times she was almost asleep on her feet. Maggie saw her through the day's work, though every now and again she gave her arm a jog. "Wake up, Kirsty! Tak' care ye dinna fall into the spindles! Here comes Mr. Murdoch! Watch or he'll lash at ye wi' the strap!"

When the whistle blew at seven-thirty, Kirsty gasped, "Can we go home now, Maggie?"

"Not till we've cleaned the machinery and swept the floor. Come on, lassie, you get awa' wi' that brush while I take the dust off the spindles."

At last they were free, to go and Kirsty stumbled along from Bridgeton to the Trongate, helped by Davie. When at last they reached the close and the stair leading to their room, she sat down weakly.

"Oh, Davie, my legs willna carry me up all those stairs!"

"I'll get my father to carry ye up," Davie said.

By the time James Murray set her down on the bed, Kirsty was already fast asleep. Kate was unwilling to waken her at 4.30 next morning, but it had to be done if the children were to be at work in time.

"Your porridge is ready, Kirsty, but will ye manage to get to the mill to-day?" Kate asked anxiously.

"Yes, I'll manage," Kirsty said in a weary voice. "Maggie Hunter says you get used to it as ye go on. Besides, you'll need our wages."

"Aye, my lassie, more's the pity!" Kate said unhappily. "It's a sad day when we've got to depend on our bairns for our bread. It was never like that at Culmailie."

In the months that followed the children got more hardened to work in the mill, though Kirsty became pale and thin and lost some of her gay spirit. Their wages at least paid the rent and kept the family in oatmeal and salt herring and cheese. Mr. McLaren was able to find Kate work cleaning in a big house for a shilling a week. Sometimes the lady for whom she worked gave her left-over food and that helped too, though there was never quite enough money for all their needs. Every now and again James had to dip into their small store of money to buy things like shoes, for the children could not run barefoot as they had done at Culmailie, though they often worked barefoot in the mill.

Once the children were in danger of losing their jobs at the mill. It happened one morning when Kirsty had chilblains on her feet and could not run. As they approached the mill they heard the big bell that meant everyone had to be inside and ready to start work. The door was just closed as they reached the mill, but Davie, greatly daring, thrust it open, hoping they would be able to reach their places without the overseer noticing them. It so happened he was standing where Kirsty would have to pass him.

"Late, are ye?" he shouted, "Trying to sneak past me, were you?" The strap descended heavily on Kirsty's thin shoulders. Davie clenched his fists and rushed up to the overseer. "Don't you dare touch my sister again!" he cried.

The overseer's arm was raised threateningly to strike Davie too but Kirsty came between them imploringly. "Please, sir, dinna strike Davie! It was my fault we were late. I've got a sore foot."

"I'll teach you to hold up your fists to me, lad!" the overseer shouted, but just then there was a shriek from another part of the mill. "Tom Paton's got his arm caught in the machinery!"

The overseer rushed away to stop the machine and release the child, and Kirsty pulled Davie by the arm. "Come, Davie! Quick to our places! We canna afford to lose our work here."

Luckily for them the overseer was so occupied in getting the injured lad away that he forgot about the boy who had defied him.

Kate was worried about other matters too, besides the hard life her children had to lead. Desperate characters lived in their part of the city.

"I've been thinking, James, is it safe for you to carry our money in your belt? Suppose you were set on by thieves? There was a young man robbed in the Trongate only last week."

"Where will I put it, then?" James asked. "Shall I hide it among the straw in the mattress?"

"That would be the first place a thief would look. There are times when we're all out of the house, when I'm cleaning for Mistress Houston and you're looking for work. Would you no' be better to give the money into the keeping of someone you can trust?"

"And who could I trust?"

"What about Mr. McLaren, the minister?"

"Why, yes, that's a good notion. I'll ask him to keep the money for us," James agreed.

Mr. McLaren hesitated at first, then at last he said, "Very well, on condition that if my house is burgled, you do not hold me responsible for your money."

"I'll take that risk, sir," James said, and then wrote down his name and address for the minister again.

Now and again James got work helping to unload small ships at the Broomielaw, mainly cargoes of potatoes from Ireland, but once the potato harvest was over the work finished, and James was unemployed again, with the winter coming on. It proved a hard winter for the Murrays, for Kate was taken ill. She lay coughing in the box bed.

"Shall I bring a doctor to you, lass?" James asked anxiously.

"You know we canna afford one, James. I'll be all right soon. Put the kettle on and give me a warm drink to ease the cough."

James lifted the kettle. "We're oot o' water again!" he

cried in exasperation. "Dear knows what I'd give for that spring o' clear water at our door at Culmailie, instead o' that well in the Trongate where there's always a long tail o' folk waiting their turn to draw."

"I'll go fetch some," Kirsty offered. Davie was out already trying to beg some firewood from a joiner's shop. Kirsty ran downstairs carrying the bucket.

"Give me a shout when ye're at the foot of the stairs and I'll carry it up," her father called after her. He did not like to leave Kate, whose eyes were bright with fever. They settled down to wait for Kirsty's return.

"Kirsty's a long time gone," Kate said at last in a weak whisper.

"Here comes someone now," James said.

It was Davie, carrying a bundle of wood. "Where's Kirsty?" he asked when he saw she was not in the room.

"Gone to the Trongate well to draw water. She's been gone a long time and I could not leave your mother."

"I'll go find her," Davie said at once. He hurried down the stair again and along the Trongate. There was a crowd of children at the well all waiting to draw water. Several of the small girls were weeping. Davie found Kirsty near the end of the queue, tears streaming from her eyes.

"Jings! Is that as far as you've got, Kirsty? What's the matter?"

"It's Tam Sweeney and those lads with him," Kirsty sobbed. "As soon as the girls get their turn at the well-head, they push and jostle us and make us go to the end of the line again. Twice I've had my bucket filled and they've turned it upside down and—and the water's getting awful low in the well."

Davie knew that when there was a run on the well it sometimes went dry and took a long time to fill again. His mother *must* have water. Davie was desperate. He strode up to the Irish bully, Tam Sweeney.

"Tam Sweeney, you let my sister go up to the well at once!" he demanded. "Did you upset her bucket before?"

Tam Sweeney eyed him up and down. "Faith, look at the young turkey cock we've got here! Sure now, and if I did, what are *you* going to do about it?"

"Think shame of yourself for tormenting bit lassies!" Davie's mouth curled in contempt. "Ye'll let my sister go to the well or——"

"Or what? You canna make me do anything!" Sweeney aimed a kick at Davie, but Davie saw it coming and jumped back. Then he sprang at Sweeney and landed a blow fairly and squarely on Tam Sweeney's nose that brought water to his eyes. His nose began to bleed.

"A fecht! A fecht!" the crowd of youths with Sweeney cried in delight. "Go for him, Sweeney!"

Tam Sweeney roared in pain and anger, "I'll break every bone in your body, you young spalpeen!"

He rushed at Davie, but Davie side-stepped quickly, dodged round Sweeney and thumped him in the ribs.

"Wait now!" A youth stepped forward. "Let's have a proper fecht. Make a ring round them both. Now, off wi' your jackets! Give them to someone to hold."

Davie saw Kirsty, white-faced, on the edge of the circle. Beside her was Maggie Hunter, her work-mate in the mill. "Here, take my jacket, Kirsty!" he said.

"Oh, Davie, Tam Sweeney's much bigger than you! Dinna be fighting him," Kirsty begged.

"If I don't fight him, all that mob will be at me and give me a beating," Davie said. "Don't be feart, Kirsty. I'll worstle through! You make a dash for the well and fill your bucket and get home with it while they're busy watching me," he added in a low voice. "Mother needs that water badly."

"Aye, Kirsty, do that! Give me Davie's jacket to hold," Maggie advised.

77

"On ye go, and no holds barred!" the tall youth cried to Tam and Davie.

Sweeney was more cautious now and advanced on Davie with upraised fists, stepping from one side to another. Davie side-stepped with him, playing for time, trying to avoid serious injury, so that Kirsty could draw her bucket of water and get away with it. Round and round the ring they went! Davie landed a light blow that grazed Sweeney's cheek, and Sweeney scored a hit on Davie's shoulder that sent him staggering, though he did not fall.

"Go it, Sweeney!" shouted the mob of boys, mostly Irish. "Give the Highlander a thrashing!"

A few more light blows were struck by both, then, with a swinging blow, Sweeney cut Davie's cheek just below his eye. Blood streamed from the cut. Davie backed away and the bully followed him. Suddenly Davie stopped dead in his tracks and Sweeney could not stop his own onward rush. Davie landed a blow square to Sweeney's chin which jarred the Irish boy's teeth and sent him staggering backwards.

"See that! The Highlander's a bonnie fechter!" a boy yelled.

"Go it, Highlander!" the mob yelled, always ready to change over to the winning side.

Sweeney shook his head like a bewildered animal for a moment, then he rushed at Davie with a roar of rage. Davie did his best to defend himself, but Sweeney rained blow after blow upon him.

"Sweeney's too good for him!" yelled Sweeney's friend. "Go it, Tam!"

Round and round the ring the two boys went, milling backwards and forwards. One of Davie's eyes was almost closed and his nose was bleeding too. Only sheer courage kept him on his feet. They were close to the ring of spectators when Sweeney made an ugly rush at Davie.

Maggie Hunter had pushed her way to the front of the

78

crowd and was watching her opportunity. As Sweeney rushed at Davie, her foot shot out. The big Irish lout tripped over it, staggered and went sprawling to the ground.

"Sweeney's down! Sweeney's down!" the mob shouted.

Sweeney pulled himself up, panting and winded with his fall.

"Someone tripped me up!" He glared at the circle of faces. "It was that lass there!" He lifted his fist menacingly at Maggie Hunter.

"Awa' wi' ye!" Maggie yelled back at him, but taking care to get behind two boys. "Dinna mak' *me* your excuse if ye canna stay on your feet!"

"I'll pull the hair from your head!" Sweeney cried, making a snatch at her. Davie realized Maggie's danger.

"Hi, you! The fight's still on!" he cried, and rushed at Sweeney who was off his guard. Davie launched a blow with the last of his strength behind it, a blow which landed just above the big bully's heart. Sweeney, already winded by his fall, doubled up completely and sat down on the ground.

"Sweeney's out! Sweeney's out! The Highlander's knocked Sweeney out!" the shout went up, and someone in the crowd began to count, "One, two, three—"

Suddenly there was a yell from the outskirts of the crowd. "Look out, lads! Here comes the Watch!"

The crowd scattered as if by magic as two stalwart figures, armed with truncheons, came at a smart pace along the street. Even Sweeney managed to pick himself up and hang on to a friend's arm and melt away round a corner. Only Davie and Maggie were left to face 'the Watch', the early police force of the Glasgow of 1813.

"What's going on here?" the bigger of the two men asked in a Highland voice. He took Davie by the shoulder.

"It was that Tam Sweeney who set on him," Maggie

79

spoke up at once. "Sweeney wouldna let the lassies draw water at the well and Davie tried to stop him."

"Och! So Sweeney has been up to his tricks again!" the watchman said angrily. "Was it the wild Irish that set on ye, lad?"

"Weel, I—I fought him back," Davie answered truthfully.

"If Davie hadna defended himself the Irish lads would have torn him limb from limb," Maggie declared.

"Ye've no business to be fechting in the street," the watchman told Davie sternly. "You could be put in gaol for that." He eyed Davie's battered face. "Ye've taken a pasting yourself, by the looks of it, laddie."

"Tam Sweeney didna get off free, either," Maggie remarked proudly.

A glint came into the Highland policeman's eye. "Did he no'? Maybe I'll no' be saying anything more about it, then. I ken those Irish!"

Just then James Murray came running round the corner. "Davie, are ye all right?" he gasped, looking at Davie's injured face with consternation.

"He's no' as bad as he looks!" the watchman said. "Take tha lad home." He turned to Davie with an assumed expression of anger, "Mind ye, if I catch ye fechting those wild Irish again, it'll be the worse for ye." Then he gave a chuckle. "It's lucky for you I'm a Highlander myself!"

James hurried Davie along in the direction of their close, with Maggie Hunter running alongside them. "What are you doing, getting mixed in a fight?" he asked Davie sternly.

Maggie spoke up. "Dinna blame him! It was because Tam Sweeney wouldna let Kirsty tak' water from the well, and Davie knew his mother sore needed it."

James's face softened.

"I'll be leaving ye noo," Maggie said, skipping off in the direction of her own home.

"Thank you for the way you helped me, Maggie," Davie called after her.

Kate Murray sat up in bed and cried at the sight of Davie's bruised face.

"It's all right, Mother. It'll look a lot better after I've washed it. You should see Tam Sweeney's!" he could not help adding.

Kirsty had told her mother of the cause of the fight. Kate, weak with illness, began to weep. "Oh, why did we have to come to this terrible city? At Culmailie we did not have to live on bread earned by our children, nor stay in a dirty place like this one! There, a stream of pure water ran past our door, and we did not have to stand in a line to draw water from a muddy well. Our children were not set upon by brutes there. Oh, why did we ever leave Culmailie?"

"Now, Kate, you know we had to leave," James told her gently. "We had no choice. You're sick and that's why your heart fails you, my poor lass."

"James, will you take us back to the Highlands when I'm strong enough to go?" Kate begged him.

"I'll do what I can, lass, though there is no living for us in the Highlands, either," James said, shaking his head in despair.

It was then that the knock came at the door.

5. A WAY IS FOUND

JAMES Murray opened the door. In a flash his look of caution changed to one of welcome, and his hand was outstretched.

"Why, it's Donald Rae, no less!" he cried with joy. "Come in, man, come in! Ye're right welcome."

The old drover stepped into the room. "My duty to you, Mistress Murray. My, but it's sorry I am to see you in your bed! You look right ill, lassie."

"Aye, Kate has not thrown off a sickness to her chest. These Glasgow fogs have been over much for her," James told him.

"The bairns are a thought peelie-wallie too," Rae remarked. "Ye'll be missing the hills about Culmailie."

"Indeed we are, Mr. Rae," Kate said huskily.

"How did you find us here?" James asked.

Donald Rae looked rather pleased with himself. "Weel, man, I used my intelligence. Ye were brought up to go to church, so I thought I'd ask a minister or two if they kenned you. A Highland minister was the most likely."

"Mr. McLaren of the Ingram Street Church!" James exclaimed.

"Aye, I was lucky the first shot! He knew you, and what was more he had your address in that wee book o' his, and when he knew why I was seeking ye, he gave it me willingly. Man, I have brought ye a letter and some money."

"A letter? Money? Is it from John at Dornoch?"

"It is, indeed! He's sold your furniture for ye, James, and he's no' done badly. It seems a lady in a big house took a fancy to that old blanket kist o' yours, Mistress Murray. She gave John ten pounds for it."

"Ten pounds for my kist that was so old!" Kate exclaimed.

"Aye, mistress. It was because it was so old. An antique, she called it. He didna do badly wi' your other furniture, either. Nineteen pounds altogether!"

"With what the minister is holding for me, that's thirty-nine pounds! Why, it's riches!" James exclaimed.

"In Glasgow it would melt like snow off a dyke and you not in work. Oh, James, let us go back to the Highlands," Kate implored.

Donald Rae frowned a little. "I would not advise that. There are more and more crofts standing empty and burned in the north."

"If I stay another winter in Glasgow, I shall die!" Kate cried.

"You have not read your brother's letter yet. See what he has to say, then I will count out the money to you," Donald advised.

James opened the letter, scanned it, then read it aloud for Kate.

"Dear Brother James,

I hope that this finds you and your family in the best of health.

I sold the furniture at a good price and I have made a list for you of the amount I got for each piece.

Did you find employment in Glasgow? We hear tales that work is hard to come by in the city.

I have a message for you from old Donald McKay of Kildonan who was with the Hudson's Bay Company in Canada. It is that Canada might be a fine place for a man like you, for it is a good healthy country with a fine soil. The Earl of Selkirk is asking for settlers for the Red River Colony where he has bought land from the Hudson's Bay Company. He will take a hundred people, men, women and children. He wishes to take families out there. There will be

a ship sailing from Stromness in Orkney to take the settlers
and the fare will be ten pounds per person and less for
children. Will you think of it, James? Donald McKay says
he will speak in your favour to the Earl of Selkirk, so I have
asked him to put your name forward. If you do not wish to
go, it can be withdrawn.

The burnings and destruction of the crofts continue. It
has been bad in Kildonan.

My thoughts are with you and Kate and your children.

Your brother,
John."

"Canada?" James added with doubt in his voice.

"Canada? Is it not a land of ice and snow, with bears
and wolves roaming free?" Kate asked.

"True! There is plenty of snow in winter, but grand
summers they have. Donald McKay said it could be a
wonderful land for farming," Rae said.

"Bears and wolves!" Davie's eyes sparkled. "Donald
McKay told me how he used to go hunting bears and
wolves for their furs. I'd like fine to be a hunter."

"What about you, my lassie?" Donald Rae smiled at
Kirsty.

"I do not know," she answered honestly. "But if Davie
wishes to go, then I would go too."

"Bravely spoken! It's a good offer, James. I would think
weel before rejecting it," Rae advised.

"But you said the ship would be sailing from the Orkney
Isles. How would we get from here to Stromness?" James
asked.

"There is a ship sails from Leith to Stromness. Leith is
less than a day's journey away if you get the carrier to take
you in his cart," Rae told him. "Once you reach Stromness,
the rest is easy. You have but to wait for the sailing of the
Hudson's Bay Company's ship for Canada."

"But the fares?" James asked. "Our little hoard of money

would not cover them, and we should need cattle and tools for farming once we got there."

"Listen, man! The Earl of Selkirk has arranged for that. He will pay £20 each year for three years to every man. What is more, he will lend you supplies and tools for a year. You can begin to pay him back when your land begins to yield its crops."

"That's fair enough," James agreed. "But shall we just be tenants of the Earl's lands? Could the same thing happen there that happened at Culmailie, that we could be turned out?"

"No, James! You will own your land. The Earl will let you buy it at five shillings an acre."

"My! That would be a bargain!" James was beginning to look interested. "But it's raising the money for the fares that would bother me."

"Ah, weel! Let me be paying the money due to you," Rae said. "There is the nineteen pounds for your furniture and here is ten pounds over and above it."

"Ten pounds!" James gasped. "Where has that come from?"

"It is from your brother John. He found your mother had money saved in an old stocking hidden in the loft. It came to light after you were away, so he sent you the half of it."

James looked overcome. "John's a fine brother!" He turned to Kate. "Weel, Kate, what do you say about Canada?"

"Are there hills in Canada like there were at Culmailie?"

"Aye, Mistress Murray, hills in plenty and grand rivers and lakes teeming with fish, so Donald Mackay said," Rae told her.

"Fish!" Davie exclaimed. "D'ye hear that, father?"

"Aye, Davie." James Murray looked as eager as his son.

"It would be grand to have a boat again and the oars in my hands."

"It would be canoes and paddles we'd have there, like the Indians," Davie replied, his eyes lighting up at the thought.

"Shall we go, Kate?" James asked his wife. "It would be the chance to start a new life. There I could live like a man and no' have to depend on my children for my bread."

She looked at him with understanding. "Aye, James, if you wish it, we'll go."

Donald Rae gave a chuckle. "It's as weel ye've decided that way, as the Earl of Selkirk has already said he'd accept ye on McKay's recommendation. There's nothing to stop ye now."

A fortnight later the ship from Leith sailed into Stromness harbour with the Murray family aboard. The three-masted *Prince of Wales* belonging to the Hudson's Bay Company was lying by the quay with some of the settlers already aboard her. It did not take the Murrays long to transfer their bundles on to the ship and to be allotted their bunks. There were a hundred folk bound for the Earl of Selkirk's new colony on the Red River, many of them families with children. Their leaders were a young man, Archibald McDonald, who had studied medicine, and a doctor, Doctor LaSerre.

At last the *Prince of Wales* set sail for Hudson's Bay and the Company's trading post at York Factory. The voyage was likely to be a long and perilous one among the ice-floes of the Arctic waters.

With sad eyes the emigrants watched the last of Scotland fall away behind them; first the roofs of Stromness sloping up to the high ground behind; then, as the sails filled under a light easterly breeze, the hills of Hoy faded from blue to purple and were lost in the grey of the sea.

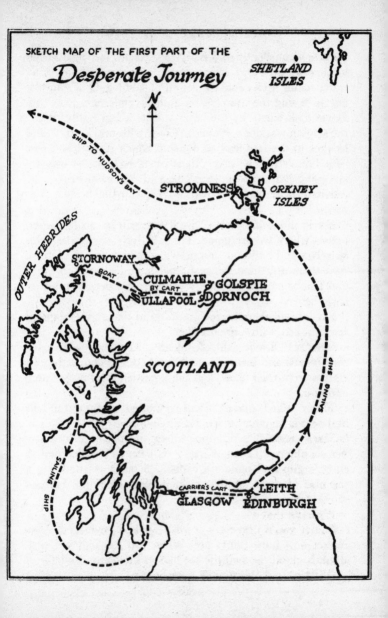

SKETCH MAP OF THE FIRST PART OF THE

Desperate Journey

SHETLAND ISLES

N

SHIP TO HUDSON'S BAY

STROMNESS

ORKNEY ISLES

OUTER HEBRIDES

STORNOWAY

BOAT

CULMAILIE

BY CART

ULLAPOOL

DORNOCH

GOLSPIE

SCOTLAND

SAILING SHIP

SAILING SHIP

CARRIER'S CART

GLASGOW

LEITH

EDINBURGH

Kate wept silently and Kirsty buried her face against her mother as the land faded from their view. From other watchers on deck came the sound of sobbing, then someone began to sing the 23rd Psalm and the emigrants joined in. Davie took Kirsty by the hand and joined in lustily. When the singing was done, he said, "Come with me, Kirsty," and led her to the forepeak of the ship which dipped and rose as it breasted each wave. "It is better to look the way we are going than to look back," he said. "Remember?"

Kirsty held back her tears. "Will Canada be like Culmailie?"

Davie shook his head. "No. There will be no fields and houses where we are going. We shall have to dig the fields ourselves and build our houses with wood out of the forests. And there are these things I shall have to learn; to fire a gun and to paddle a canoe, and to drive a sledge pulled by dogs."

"What will there be for me to do in that strange land?" Kirsty asked a little doubtfully.

"Plenty!" Davie said confidently. "You'll have to cook the animals and birds we shall shoot for the pot, and make clothes from their skins, and dig a garden to grow potatoes and kail."

Kirsty pulled a face. "Shall we not get roaming the hills and woods together as we did at Culmailie?"

Davie sensed her disappointment and put an arm across her shoulders. "Listen, Kirsty! As soon as I've learned to shoot a gun and handle a canoe, I'll teach you too. It's a promise. Haven't we always done things together? Promise me one thing, though, Kirsty."

"What's that?"

"That you'll never say 'I wish we had never come', no matter how hard things are. When you feel like saying it, think back on the bad life we had in the cotton mill."

"I'll do that, Davie, only stick by me."

"I'll stick by you, never fear!" Davie promised for his part.

As the ship ploughed her way west by north, the strong winds blew. The hundred passengers were packed below decks, two to a bunk. Families kept together as much as they could. Kirsty shared a bunk with her mother and Davie with his father. There was no privacy except by nailing curtains and sailcloth across their bunks.

Ventilation was poor, for port holes had to be closed against the salt spray. Right from the start of the voyage most of the passengers were terribly sea-sick. They lay in their bunks moaning and retching, Kirsty and her mother among them.

Davie spent most of his time on deck. Everything about the ship was a joy to him. He struck up a friendship with a sailor, Tom Peterson, who taught him how to splice a rope and reef a sail. On board were several members of the Hudson's Bay Company returning from a visit to Britain. These men did not share the emigrants' cabins but had their own cabin on deck. Among them was a sturdy bearded man, his face tanned by sun and wind. His good-natured smile attracted Davie.

"Who is that man? He is not one of our people going out to Red River, is he?" Davie asked Tom.

"No. That's Robert Finlay. He's one of the factors of the Hudson's Bay Company."

The only factor Davie knew was the hated Patrick Sellar. "Surely that man does not collect rents?" he asked Peter.

Peter laughed aloud. "No' that kind of factor, laddie! Mr. Finlay is in charge of one of the trading posts."

"Trading posts?"

"Aye. The Indians bring in the furs from the animals they trap and Mr. Finlay gives them goods in exchange."

Davie looked at the tough trader with admiration. "Indians! Furs! Guid sakes! My! I wish I could talk to him!"

Almost as if the wind heard his wish, a sudden gust lifted the trader's fur cap from his head. Davie was after it like a flash and pounced on it just as it reached the scuppers by the deck rail. He carried it back to Robert Finlay.

"Well caught, lad! I'm much obliged to you," Finlay said. "My favourite cap, that!" He looked at Davie's eager face smiling at him. "Came off the first silver fox I ever trapped," he told Davie. "Are you one of the emigrant children?"

"Yes, sir."

"Your name, lad?"

"David Murray."

"You think you'll like the life in Canada, lad?"

"Oh, yes, sir! Maybe I'll get a boat or a canoe on the Red River and be able to go fishing."

"It'll be a hard tough life, Davie. It won't be all fishing. You'll have to work on the land too."

"Yes, sir. I've helped my father before on his farm."

Just then there was a shout from Tom Peterson who pointed out to sea. A ship was approaching under heavy sail.

"Here comes a whaler!" Mr. Finlay exclaimed. "They'll have been whale hunting in the Davis Strait."

"How do you know the ship's a whaler, sir?" Davie asked.

Robert Finlay laughed. "Sniff the wind, lad! The wind's bringing a smell of whale oil and blubber. There'll be a right stench aboard."

"It couldna be worse than the stench below decks on this ship," Davie remarked candidly. "It's awful down there with everyone being sea-sick."

"They'll get over that before long. If folk would come up on deck into the clean air, they'd feel a lot better."

"My mother and sister have been pretty bad," Davie said soberly. "Why! Here's Father with Kirsty now," he exclaimed as they appeared on deck. "Are you feeling any better, Kirsty?"

"I don't think I *can* be sick any more," Kirsty declared.

"You'll be better for a breath of air, my lassie," Mr. Finlay smiled at her. He turned to James Murray. "Are you the father of this pair?"

"Aye, sir, they're twins. My name's James Murray."

"Are there many sick folk below?"

"I think the worst of the sea-sickness is over, but folk are terribly weak and there are one or two folk who look fevered."

Finlay gave him a sharp look. "Fevered, did you say? Mr. Murray, you seem a sensible man. If you'll take my advice, you'll keep your family on deck as much as you can, even to sleep there, if possible."

"Will it no' be very cold, sir?"

"Wrap yourself well round with blankets and ye'll be none the worse. You may find it gets too cold when we reach the ice-fields, but by then the sickness below should have abated."

"Icefields!" Davie exclaimed. "Shall we be going among the ice? Will there be icebergs?"

"Most likely!" Robert Finlay laughed, "and before long too!"

That very night the winds blew colder, but the Murray family, huddled under their blankets in the shelter of one of the lifeboats and covered by a piece of sail-cloth that Tom Peterson found for them, slept sounder than they had done for nights in the foul-smelling cabin. Then, one day, when they reached the Davis Strait, they woke to a white fog and the sound of the ship's bell clanging. The sails hung limply without a breath of wind to give them a flap. David and Kirsty went forward and hung over the rail, trying to see through the woolly whiteness ahead. They were joined by Mr. Finlay.

Davie ventured a question. "Is the ship's bell sounding to warn other ships we are near, sir?"

Finlay shook his head. "Not likely to be many ships around here! No, they're sounding to get an echo."

"An echo?"

"Aye, off the side of an iceberg. This fog is caused by an iceberg in the neighbourhood which is chilling the warmer air. If we get an echo, we shall know the iceberg is close to us."

"Oh, Kirsty, maybe we'll see an iceberg!" Davie exclaimed in delight.

"Let's hope we *do* see it in plenty of time!" Finlay remarked.

Kirsty opened her eyes wide. "Why, sir, is it dangerous?"

Before Robert Finlay had time to reply, the sound of the bell began to echo, at first distantly, then louder and louder, till the echo was almost as distinct as the bell.

"It's getting very near to us now," the trader remarked.

"Is the iceberg *moving*?" Davie asked in surprise.

"Aye, Davie, it's being brought towards us on the current."

Finlay could not disguise the anxiety in his voice. "Step back, children, under the shelter of the boat," he said sharply, indicating one of the ship's boats that swung on its davits.

Suddenly the mists parted and the sun shone through. There, bearing down on them, was a huge mountain of ice. It carried pinnacles like a hundred cathedrals, reflecting the sun in rainbow flashes, dazzling to blindness. Majestically it sailed towards them. Fearful, yet fascinated, Kirsty shaded her eyes.

"It's beautiful!" she breathed.

Robert Finlay, beside them, watched the angle of its approach keenly. It towered above the ship.

"With luck it might miss us by a dozen yards provided it has no sharp shelves beneath the water," he said.

"Is there a lot more of the iceberg beneath the water?" Davie asked.

"Why, yes, my boy, seven times as much below as above."

From the iceberg there came a chilling cold that seemed to freeze them to the deck.

"It's sailing past us," Davie said, but hardly were the words out of his mouth than there was a horrid rasping sound and the whole ship shuddered terribly. Robert Finlay gave the children a push. "Stand under the lifeboat!" he cried. "Pray God it does not rip the hull out of our ship!"

The emigrants were most of them on deck staring at the white mountain that seemed about to topple down on the ship. Kirsty clung to Davie, white-faced, unable to speak.

There was another grating sound, and the whole ship shook again. An overhanging pinnacle of the iceberg broke off and came crashing down in a ton of broken ice just where the children had been standing a few minutes earlier, breaking the rail, even rattling upon the boat under which they were sheltering. The sudden weight of ice caused the *Prince of Wales* to heel over at a dangerous angle. Kirsty and Davie began to slide down towards the gap in the ship's rail. Kirsty shrieked in terror and clutched Davie. It seemed as if they would be flung in the icy seas. Davie was brought up against one of the iron davits to which the boat was slung. He flung out an arm and grabbed it and brought their headlong slide to a halt.

The ship seemed to pause in her roll and hung for a moment as if doubtful whether to turn turtle or not. The fearful emigrants, hanging on to anything they could grasp, held their breath, and some prayed. Then slowly, slowly, the *Prince of Wales* came back from the dreadful plunge.

Foot by foot the starboard side rose, came level, slipped a

little over to port, then gave a gentle roll back into a horizontal position once more.

"Look, Kirsty! The iceberg's well past us now!" Kirsty lifted her face from Davie's shoulder where she had hidden it in fear.

James Murray and Kate came rushing towards their children.

"Are ye hurt, bairns?" Kate asked.

"We might have been if Mr. Finlay had not told us to move to the shelter of the boat," Davie told her. "The ice came crashing on deck just where we were standing."

"Thank you indeed, sir." James Murray said to Finlay.

"What is it like below?" Finlay asked. "Is there any inrush of water into the hold?"

"I saw none."

"We shall be lucky if we have not sprung a leak," Finlay said, shaking his head.

Soon they saw the captain moving among the anxious crowds that thronged the decks, frightened to stay below.

"Calm yourselves, good folk!" he told them. "Thanks be to God the worst of the danger is over now. One of the ship's seams has sprung a leak but the sailors are already busy caulking it and a pump is dealing with the water that has got in. Pray God sends a wind soon, so that we may be able to sail on our way!"

Someone in the crowd began to sing the words of the Old Hundredth, and soon all were joining in.

"Praise God from whom all blessings flow,
Praise Him all creatures here below,
Praise Him above, ye heavenly host,
Praise Father, Son and Holy Ghost."

As the strains of the hymn died away over the waste of waters, a gentle breeze came from the south and began to fill the sails. The sea-anchor was winched up and the *Prince of Wales* began to move northward again.

A few days later the ship left the Davis Strait and turned eastward into the Hudson Strait. The next day they sighted Resolution Island off the starboard bow, with black barren cliffs tumbling to the rocky sea-beaten shore. Behind the cliffs were dreary snow-clad peaks.

"Oh, Davie, how desolate it looks! Not a tree anywhere! Will our new land look like that?" Kirsty's lips trembled a little.

Robert Finlay overheard her question. "Cheer up, my lassie! The new land will be full of trees and birds and carpeted with wild flowers in the spring. This is just the hard cheerless way you must take to reach your new land. Soon the ship will turn south again, but not before you've been through the ice-field."

Robert Finlay took Kirsty by the shoulder and pointed to the north-west. "D'ye see yon glint over by the horizon?"

Kirsty nodded. "There's a kind of shimmering white dazzle there."

"That's what we call the 'ice-glint'. It comes from the sun shining on the ice-field."

"How will the ship get through the ice-field?" Davie asked.

"There are wide cracks like gulfs through which the ship can sail or be pulled if there's not enough wind to sail her. Then the sailors take ropes and climb on the ice and warp the ship along the sea-passages."

Davie's eyes glowed. "I'd like fine to see that!"

"I wish we could see some people who live here," Kirsty said a little plaintively.

"Ye'll be doing that soon, my lassie! When we reach Ungava Bay you'll see plenty of Eskimos."

"Eskimos!" Kirsty clapped her hands in delight.

Robert Finlay was right. That night the ship sailed closer

in to the coast and next day the children were wakened by a babble of voices shouting "Chimo! Chimo! Pillattaa! Pillattaa!"

"Whatever's that?" Kirsty cried. They rushed to the rail. There were at least thirty canoes swarming round the ship. The men were in one-man kayaks made of seal-skin and the women two or three together in larger canoes. They shouted and laughed, showing strong white teeth in their flat-featured faces. The men held up their paddles in greeting and the women waved their trade-goods in the air.

"What do they want?" Kirsty asked, a little frightened of the wild shouting figures.

"They want to trade with us. The men are asking to come aboard with the things they have to sell, but the captain will only let them come aboard two or three at a time."

"Why? Would they attack us?" Kirsty asked.

"No, but they'd steal from us. Terrible thieves they are! When there's a crowd you can't keep an eye on them all."

"Don't they know it's wrong to steal?" Kirsty said.

"Bless you, no! They think it's a clever thing to steal from strangers. Here comes the first group now!"

Captain Turner allowed six of the Eskimos at a time to come up the rope ladder aboard. They brought many strange articles to trade, whalebone, necklaces made from sea-horse teeth, small models of canoes made from bones. The women showed tunics made of seal-skin and fur hoods and wraps.

The sailors then brought up their articles to barter; packets of needles, knives, beads, axes and even tin kettles. The Eskimos' eyes glittered with eagerness.

"There's a man showing a lovely little model canoe of bone," Davie said. "He's pointing to that tin kettle."

"He'll not get it for that," Robert Finlay laughed. The sailor with the tin kettle shook his head.

"Now the Eskimo is pointing to an axe," Kirsty remarked.

"He'll not get that either!"

The pointing finger moved to a knife and then to a pen-knife and there it stopped. The sailor nodded, held out the knife and the Eskimo held out the model canoe. Not till he had grasped the knife did he let go of the canoe.

"Not very trusting, is he?" Davie commented.

"It's just their way of bargaining. Watch what he does now."

"Why, he's *licked* the knife!" Kirsty cried in astonishment.

"That's his way of showing possession. Here comes a woman now! She's holding up a fur hood."

"I'd like fine to have a fur hood like that for when we go hunting, but I suppose the Eskimos would not trade with us?" Davie asked.

"Oh, yes, they will, if you've any goods to offer," Finlay said.

James Murray had joined the group round the Eskimos. "I'd buy the lad a hood if the Eskimo would take money."

"Money's no use to him, man!" Finlay laughed. "No shops in his land! Have you a comb or a bright handkerchief you could spare?"

James Murray produced a large red handkerchief with white spots from his pocket.

"Just the thing! See, yon Eskimo has his eyes on it already."

James Murray pointed to the fur cap the Eskimo held, then to the handkerchief. The Eskimo was fascinated by it. He held out the fur cap and the exchange was made.

"Here you are, Davie!" James Murray set the cap over Davie's ears. Kirsty looked just a bit wistful. An Eskimo woman was quick to see Kirsty's look and understand it. She held up a soft sealskin tunic and pointed to Kirsty.

"I think she means that tunic would fit you, Kirsty," Davie said.

G   97

"What will she take for it?" Mrs. Murray asked quickly. "I have a packet of needles in my pocket." She held them up but the woman shook her head.

"She means it is not enough," Robert Finlay said. "Have you anything else, Mrs. Murray?"

Mrs. Murray dipped into the pocket of her skirt and laid a pair of scissors alongside the needles.

"You might need those, ma'am, when you get to the Red River," Finlay advised her.

"I have two larger pairs in our luggage. I can spare these." Kate held them up and demonstrated their use by snipping a small lock from Kirsty's hair. The Eskimo woman was delighted. At once she handed over the tunic, seizing the scissors at the same time, licked them in token of ownership, and set to work to snip at her own long black hair. Kate Murray slipped the tunic over Kirsty's head.

"It's warm!" Kirsty snuggled into it.

"Well, now you've each got a garment suitable to this climate," Robert Finlay laughed.

As the ship continued her voyage, most people had recovered from sea-sickness, but several folk still lay in their bunks, too ill and fevered to eat. At first Doctor LaSerre had put this down to bad attacks of sea-sickness, till one man died, and some patients began to break out in spots. He sought out Captain Turner.

"I fear there is a worse illness than sea-sickness among our settlers," he told the captain. "One man has died and there is a child at the point of death. There is a fading rash on her body. It could be scarlet fever or—or typhus." The doctor spoke the last dread word in a low voice.

"Typhus? That could spread like fire among those folk packed below deck." The captain looked shocked.

"It could indeed," the doctor agreed.

"What measures can you take."

"I will try to keep the sick people in one cabin, but they

have already been mixing with the others. I can only look out for further suspected cases and separate them at once." The doctor staggered slightly as he spoke.

"Are *you* all right, man?" the captain asked sharply.

"It is nothing. Perhaps I am rather tired. There have been so many sick people to look after. If—if I should be taken ill," the doctor stammered, "there is a young man among the Highlanders, one of their leaders, Archibald McDonald, who has been apprenticed to a doctor though he is not yet one. He has been helping me—helping me—" the doctor faltered, then he spun round and crashed in a heap.

That night Dr. LaSerre was in a high fever, muttering and delirious. As the ship passed into Hudson's Bay, he died. Five other emigrants died too. Archibald McDonald found he had thirty typhus patients on his hands! Fear spread among the emigrants: every man eyed his neighbour for the suspicious signs of the dreaded disease. Kate Murray watched her children anxiously.

"Pray God we have not brought our bairns on this terrible journey, to die of a fever before we have reached our promised land," she said to her husband.

"Keep a good heart, Kate. Davie and Kirsty have lived on deck more than any other children in the ship. Mr. Finlay says the fever cannot live in the open air. We will keep ourselves to ourselves as much as we can." Kate Murray looked thoughtful as her husband said this.

Archibald McDonald turned one cabin into a sick bay and there he sent everyone who showed any sign of the fever. He called for volunteers among the women to help to nurse the sick. Kate was torn between care for her own children and a feeling that she *must* help with the sick and dying. At last she told her husband, "James, I know we said we would keep ourselves apart, but if I do not do my duty and help with the sick, it will be on my conscience for the rest of my days."

"What if you bring the disease to our children?" James asked.

"I have thought about that. Those who are helping with the sick are keeping apart from the rest. I shall not come near you till we land at York Factory. It will be hard, but better so. No, do not look at me so doubtfully. There are children that need nursing, James. Suppose they were our own?"

"But you, Kate? What about you?" James looked troubled.

"With God's grace I shall hope to be spared. Mr. McDonald must have helpers."

"Could he no' find helpers among the families with sick people?" Davie asked, when he heard what his mother meant to do.

"Davie, this colony that we are going to make in this new land—" his mother looked at him very earnestly. "—It can only live and grow if we all help each other. If we fail each other now we shall never stand shoulder to shoulder when we are threatened by even greater dangers. That is why I must do what I can."

Davie nodded. "Yes, I understand that, Mother."

"Because I do not wish to risk giving you the fever, I shall keep apart from you all and live in the nurses' quarters."

"Oh, Mother!" Kirsty looked dismayed.

"Keep a good heart, Kirsty, and look after your father and brother for me. It may not be for long."

"Your wife is a brave woman, James Murray," Finlay said when he heard what Kate had done. "It takes courage above the ordinary to tackle a thing like that. You and your family are the right stuff to make good settlers. If I can help you to look after your children, man, I will."

A day later they reached the floating ice-field. There was only one channel through it, and as the ship took it, the ice closed round her, hemming her in. Kirsty looked fearfully at the dazzling whiteness round them.

"Will the ship be held tight for ever, Davie?"

"No, I do not think so. There is already a warmer wind blowing from the south," Mr. Finlay answered for Davie. "It will open up the cracks in the ice yet, and the captain says with his spy-glass he can see a stretch of wide water beyond. As soon as the channel opens the sailors will warp the ship along with ropes to the end of it."

"That'll be a grand sight!" Davie exclaimed.

"Aye, lad, but before then, if I'm not mistaken, we'll have some other kind of sport." Mr. Finlay had been looking through his spy-glass. He handed it to Davie. "What do you make those out to be?"

Davie was very proud to have the loan of the spy-glass. "Bears!" he cried, "Are they bears?"

"Aye, they're bears, three of them. How would you like to go hunting, Davie?"

Davie's eyes sparkled. "Oh, do you mean it, Mr. Finlay?"

"I'm going to ask Captain Turner if he can spare me a boat and a couple of men to row and I'll take my musket. Would you like to come too?"

"Oh, yes!" Davie replied eagerly.

James Murray was no less keen. "If—if you needed someone to row, Mr. Finlay, I know how to handle a boat," then he said in a disappointed voice, "Oh, but there's Kirsty! I'd better stay with her now her mother—"

"Oh, but I overheard Kirsty telling Davie she wanted to learn how to handle a gun too," Robert Finlay's blue eyes twinkled. "Maybe we should let Kirsty come along in the boat with us?"

"Oh, please, Mr. Finlay." Kirsty went pink with eagerness.

"Right! Then go put on all the warm clothes you've got while I make matters right with the captain, and see if he'll loan me Mr. Cotterell, the first mate, and Tom Peterson to go along with us."

The captain was quite willing to allow a boat to be launched. Davie and Kirsty climbed down the rope ladder while Tom Peterson and Mr. Cotterell held the boat steady. She and Davie huddled together in the stern of the boat while the four men each took an oar. A number of people watched them from the ship's side.

The men pulled the boat well up the channel. "We must get up beyond the bears so that the wind does not carry our scent to them," Robert Finlay explained.

As they drew nearer they saw the group of bears comprised a she-bear and two cubs. The cubs were frolicking about on the ice, pretending to fight each other, while the mother-bear gave each of them a gentle cuff with her paw when they got too rough.

The boat pulled in to the ice bank and Mr. Finlay stepped on to it with his musket, followed by Mr. Cotterell and James Murray. Mr. Finlay gave Kirsty a helping hand on to the ice. Tom Peterson stayed behind in the boat so that it should not drift away and leave them marooned.

"Move very quietly and softly, a few steps at a time. Stop when you see me stop and freeze in your tracks at once," Finlay warned the party.

"Just what we're likely to do!" Davie could not help saying in a low turn to Kirsty, who giggled, then covered her mouth with her hand guiltily. Robert Finlay overheard what Davie had said and he glanced round with a frown. "Davie, you must *not* speak again if you are going with this hunting party, not even to make a joke. Silence and obedience are absolutely necessary to a hunter. I must get near enough to the bears to make a clean kill."

Davie hung his head ashamed.

They approached the bears a few steps at a time until they got within easy gunshot of them, so engrossed with their

play were the young cubs and their mother with watching
them. Mr. Finlay waved the party to draw nearer yet.

Suddenly the mother-bear looked about her uneasily. It
was as though she scented danger. She turned and saw the
group of men. At first she growled menacingly and took a
step or two towards them, then, as if she knew they were too
many for her, she retreated and growled to her cubs. They
stopped their play and tumbled over the ice to their mother,
frightened as children might be at the sudden surprise of
danger. She clasped them both within her forepaws as if she
would protect them with her own body and let out a doleful
howl. She looked at one cub and then at the other, as if she
could not make up her mind which to save. She looked
behind her for a way of retreat, but there was nothing save
the wide expanse of ice, for the men stood between her and

the water where she might find safety. One cub scrambled on to her back. Robert Finlay took a careful sighting along his musket. The bear clasped the other cub to her, then once again she gave a pitiful cry as if she were begging for mercy.

"Oh!" Kirsty moaned. Robert Finlay lowered his musket. Mr. Cotterell, the mate, did the same with his.

"I'm sorry for spoiling your shot, Mr. Finlay," Kirsty said.

Robert Finlay patted Kirsty's head. "That's all right, Kirsty. You didn't really spoil my shot. I just felt that I could not bear to kill her. She is too like a human mother with her children. How do you feel, Mr. Cotterell?"

"I couldn't have shot either, sir."

"Then you're not—not cross with me, Mr. Finlay?" Kirsty faltered.

"No, Kirsty, I'm not. There is a difference about hunting when one is in need of meat for food and furs for clothes. Then one has to hunt to kill. When it is just for sport—well, I think it is better to be merciful, and we are in no need of meat or furs just now."

As though the tension had been broken, the bear and her cubs began to shamble away from them over the ice-floe.

"Now we'd better go back to the ship," Mr. Finlay said.

When they reached the ship a warmer wind was already blowing more strongly from the south, and the ice cracked about her and began to drift away from her sides as Robert Finlay had predicted. Soon the ship was floating freely again. The channel of water widened but it was still not enough to permit of sailing. Captain Turner shouted commands from the bridge.

"We'll warp the ship along, Mr. Mate. Make two teams of men. Some of the settlers can lend the sailors a hand. Fix ropes to the forepeak of the ship, then lower two boats to take the men and the ends of the ropes to both banks of the ice. When you get there, put your teams on the ropes on each bank, then pull for all you're worth. We must get the ship free of the ice and into the wider water before the freeze-up comes again with the night."

James Murray volunteered to join a team, and after him, like his shadow, went Davie. Kirsty stayed behind on deck to watch. Soon the two teams were assembled on each bank of the ice and the men took the strain of the ropes. On deck the ship's fiddler began to tune his fiddle. He was joined by a Highland piper, Donald Gunn, one of the emigrants. Together they began to play one of the famous pulling and warping shanties that had been sung by British sailors for many a long year. Tom Peterson's strong voice rang out, leading the singing.

"I sing you a song of the ships of the sea,"

He was answered by the chorus of the men on the ropes.

"'Way down Rio!"

"I sing you a song of the ships of the sea,"

"And we're bound for the Rio Grande!" boomed the chorus.

In time to each beat of the music they hauled on the rope, swayed, paused and hauled again, a beautiful rhythmic movement. The people on deck joined in the singing too, and the ship moved gracefully over the grey water of the narrow gulf, pulled by the men she had sheltered and brought so far in safety. When she reached the wide safe water going to the open sea of Hudson's Bay, the music ended; the men came back on board, and the ship shook out her sails like a lovely bird poised for flight.

6. THE TRAIL TO THE RED RIVER

THE typhus fever still claimed its victims, and though some sick people recovered, it was plain that others would never reach the new colony. Every day Kate Murray came at a fixed time to the door of the cabin given up to the fever patients and waved to her family to show them she was still well.

"Thank God your mother has not taken the sickness!" James told Kirsty, but neither of them dared say a word of the fear in their hearts.

Archibald McDonald, the leader of the Sutherlanders, wondered when the danger of infection would be over. So did Captain Turner. He sent for McDonald and, with Mr. Cotterell, the mate, he talked to him about the sickness.

"I have never had this fever in my ship before. Already you have lost a number of settlers and I have lost two reliable lads from my crew," he told McDonald. "If I lose any more men, how am I to sail my ship home again? I cannot easily pick up seafaring men in the Arctic."

"Maybe there will be one or two men of the Hudson's Bay Company willing to work their passage home," Cotterell suggested.

Captain Turner frowned at him. "I cannot rely on that. I would like to get this load of settlers landed as soon as may be. The fever patients would be better where they can be kept apart from the others. I mean to make for Fort Churchill which is nearer than York Factory and set the passengers ashore there."

Both McDonald and Cotterell looked at him in surprise. "But the settlers are not expected at Fort Churchill, sir. Will there be provision for them?" McDonald asked.

Captain Turner shrugged his shoulders. "There must be

some provisions there. In any case, your settlers will have to learn to get their meat by hunting it, will they not?"

"Aye, sir once they are quite fit," McDonald agreed, "but at present many of them are so weak that I doubt if they could stand on their feet. Had you not better carry us on to York Factory?"

York Factory was the principal trading post and port of the Hudson's Bay Company.

"There are plenty of fit people left to hunt meat for the rest," the captain declared. "It is the season when many partridges fly over. Besides, there will be stores at Fort Churchill which the Company will allow you to buy."

"Buy? My people have not much money, sir, and they will need to buy animals and seeds for their farms when we reach the colony."

"They would have had to buy food at York Factory just the same, the Captain argued.

"But it is at York Factory we are *expected*," McDonald protested.

The Captain grew annoyed. "Young man, you must allow me to judge what is best for my ship. I shall put in at Fort Churchill."

So the *Prince of Wales* headed to the west instead of to the south.

Robert Finlay was also concerned when he found they were not to be landed at York Factory, and he went to Captain Turner to remonstrate with him, but it was plain that Captain Turner was not to be stirred.

The ship sailed on towards Fort Churchill. As they passed Eskimo Point, the emigrants crowded at the rails to get a first glimpse of the shores of their new land. Their faces fell when they saw the icy bleakness and the barren rocks crowned by the forbidding buildings of the Fort.

"It looks like a prison!" Davie exclaimed.

"Will—will the place where we are to live look like this?"

Kirsty faltered. Even James Murray looked at the land in dismay.

"Cheer up! Your new home lies nearly seven hundred miles to the south. It is much warmer there, and in spring lovely flowers bloom on the prairies," Robert Finlay spoke encouragement.

"But how shall we get there?" Davie asked.

"Oh, by canoe part of the way."

"Canoe!" Davie exclaimed in delight.

"But you'll have some quite long stretches to cover on foot too," Finlay warned them. "You may even have to go on snowshoes part way."

The ship drew into the berth by the great Fort and then began the work of taking the passengers ashore. The sick people had to be lowered on home-made stretchers made of a piece of sail-cloth lashed to poles. Kirsty looked anxiously for her mother.

"There she is, helping that wee child." Davie pointed.

Kate Murray came ashore carrying a small girl. As though by instinct she looked up to where her own children were standing by the rail.

"Mother! Mother!" Kirsty cried to her. Her father laid a hand on her shoulder to keep her from running down the gang-plank. He called to his wife, "Are you all right, Kate? No signs of the fever?"

"No, James. I'm well, thank God! Mr. McDonald says as soon as there are no fresh cases and a few days have gone by to make sure none of the nurses have taken the sickness, he will be able to spare some of us to return to our own families."

"Oh, Mother, I pray it will be soon!" Kirsty faltered.

"Keep a good heart, my lassie! It may not be long before I can join you again. I am not so much with the sick women now as looking after their children."

There was no shelter for the settlers at all! In compassion, the Hudson's Bay company helped the settlers to build a hut for the fever patients and to erect tents for the nurses.

"There is no place for my people to sleep," Archibald McDonald told the captain.

"You've got axes and saws in plenty and there are strong men among you, and plenty of timber in the woods. How do you think the first Hudson's Bay traders made their homes?" the captain said.

"The first traders did not have their women and children with them," McDonald answered bitterly.

"Mr. Finlay is making arrangements to help you."

"I still think the best arrangement would have been to get these people to York Factory where they were expected," Mr. Finlay told the captain plainly. "I have sent word to the officials of the Hudson's Bay Company there to tell them what has happened. Meantime we must try to fix up tents for the families, until they can erect more permanent shelters."

Davie thought it was wonderful to be living in a real Indian tent made of buffalo hide, and to boil their kettles and cook their meals over a camp fire in the open. "This is just grand. It makes me feel like a real hunter," he declared.

"Maybe! But *I'd* like a house!" Kirsty declared. "And— and I wish Mother was back with us. It's all very well for you, Davie! You can talk to men and other boys—" Her voice choked a little.

That very day, while Kirsty was making a stew of dried buffalo meat which James had bought from the fort's stores, she looked up to see her mother at the door of the tent. Kirsty jumped to her feet, dropping the knife and stew-pan.

"Mother! Mother!" she cried. "Have you come back to us for good?"

"Yes, my lassie. A number of patients have recovered and Mr. McDonald says it will be better for those who have had the disease to nurse those who are still sick, for they are not likely to take the fever again. He thought it would be safe for me to come back to my own family."

"Oh, I'm so glad, so glad!" Kirsty wept tears of thankfulness.

"Where are your father and Davie?"

"They have gone to shoot partridges for the pot."

"Partridges! My! It's only the landed folk eat partridges in Scotland!"

"It will be a change from this tough buffalo meat."

Kate looked at the meat. "I think that meat needs soaking for a long time and pounding with a hammer to make it tender, then it must be stewed slowly for a long time over the red embers of the fire."

"Everything's going to be better now you're back, Mother!" Kirsty cried thankfully.

It was a joyful reunion round their camp-fire that evening. James and Davie had brought back a brace of partridges and a hare.

"I shot one partridge myself with Mr. Finlay's gun," Davie said with pride. "He let me have a shot with it."

"My! You're a hunter already," Kate laughed.

When Miles MacDonell, the Governor of the Red River Colony, heard that Captain Turner had put the settlers ashore at Fort Churchill without food or shelter, he was furious. "I hope he will be made to smart severely for his brutal stubbornness," he told Mr. Auld, one of the chief men at York Factory.

Mr. Auld travelled to Fort Churchill to find out what was happening there and he said to Captain Turner, "You will take these wretched people on board again and carry them to York Factory."

"I cannot do that. I have to take my ship back to England at once."

"Captain Turner, I am giving you orders which must be

obeyed. If you do not obey, you will answer for it to the Company."

Grumbling, Captain Turner took the settlers aboard again.

"At last we're on our journey once more!" Kate said as they left Sloop's Cove. Hardly were the words out of her mouth than there came a terrible jarring sound and the ship shuddered from stem to stern.

"Oh, what's happening?" Kirsty cried.

White waves were curling round the bows of the ship. "I think we've run aground!" Davie exclaimed.

It was too true! The *Prince of Wales* was caught hard on a sand-bar across the harbour.

"Perhaps the ship will refloat with the tide," James Murray hoped, but high tide still saw the ship held fast.

"We shall have to lighten the ship," Captain Turner decided. "The settlers and their gear will have to be taken ashore in the ship's boats."

Mr. Auld was very angry. "Captain Turner, I have my suspicions that this grounding was no accident. You were determined not to go to York Factory."

"That is something you cannot prove, sir," the Captain retorted.

"That may be, but once the ship is refloated, you will take them aboard again!"

But that night the wind began to blow strongly and severe gales set in. It was impossible for the *Prince of Wales* to sail. After several days Mr. Auld called the settlers about him.

"I am sorry, but it will be impossible to get you to York Factory before the winter sets in. There is nothing for it but to winter here. Fifteen miles up the Churchill River there is a place with plenty of wood to build huts and make fires. You will have to fell trees, but you will have to do that anyway, when you reach the Red River."

"Some of us will never reach the Red River if we have to spend the winter here," a settler told him. "What shall we do for food?"

"Plenty of fish in the river!" Auld told him impatiently. "Most of you have guns too. If you are short of food, you are not far from Fort Churchill where you can buy pemmican meat if you fetch it on your sledges."

Pemmican was dried and powdered buffalo meat that was packed in skin sacks. It was supplied by the Indian tribes to the Hudson's Bay Company.

Those of the settlers who were fit went ahead to the place shown them on the Churchill River. They felled trees, sawed off logs and built rough timber houses by laying the logs one on top of the other and plastering the cracks with wet clay taken from the river. Davie worked alongside his father. At last the huts were ready to inhabit and the women and children came from Fort Churchill. Davie proudly showed their hut to Kirsty and Kate.

"Once you're inside, you cannot feel the wind at all. We've even made furniture, see!" He pointed to the sawn-off circular slabs of tree-trunk that did duty for tables and chairs.

"But where are the beds?" Kirsty asked.

"We've got hammocks to sling from the beams. Father bought them at Fort Churchill. We were not able to make a floor: there was no time," he told his mother a little ruefully. "We'll just have to make do with the beaten earth."

"We could gather moss and dry it," Kirsty suggested. "If we spread that on the floor, it would be warm to our feet." Already the children were beginning to think of ways of making their new life more comfortable in this strange bleak land.

At the end of September winter began to close in with bitter Arctic winds and flurries of snow. There were plenty of partridges and geese flying south and the settlers shot them for the pot. They caught fish and dried them. Sometimes the men took their sledges and went to Fort Churchill for supplies of dried buffalo meat. For Davie this was an exciting time. He came into the hut one day glowing with exercise. He had been to Fort Churchill with the men to fetch back pemmican.

"Fifteen miles there and fifteen miles back, and I easily kept up with all of them!" he told Kirsty proudly. "We went along the river ice on snowshoes."

"It's all very well for you, Davie, shooting and fishing and racing off to Fort Churchill, but what is there for me to do here except *sew*? I am tired of making fur mittens out of the hares you catch! I wish—"

"Remember, Kirsty!" Davie warned her, putting his finger to his lips. "You promised."

Kirsty snapped her lips shut, but the tears welled up. Davie looked at her with concern. "Listen, Kirsty! Why shouldn't you learn to go on snow-shoes?"

"Do you think I could?"

"You'd take a few tumbles at first, but you'd learn. Then you could go with me fishing and trapping."

"It might be as weel if we all learned to go on snow-shoes." James Murray said thoughtfully. "I was speaking to Mr. Finlay up at Fort Churchill today, and he said that when March came a party of us, the strong and fit ones, should set out over the snow for York Factory."

"Why should we do that?" Kate asked. "Will they no' send a ship to take us?"

"A ship cannot get through to us till the ice melts in the Bay. We would get to the Red River too late to plant crops for a harvest this year. Mr. Finlay says we ought to be at York Factory ready to make a start for the Red River as soon as the ice breaks on the rivers. We shall still have seven hundred miles to go on foot and by canoe. I would like us to start life together in the new colony. Will you learn to use snow-shoes, so that you will be ready to go, Kate?"

"I will do my best," she promised. "Little did I think it would be this way we'd travel to our promised land, though, James, when we set out on that first desperate journey from Culmailie."

"Aye, desperate it has been, and desperate it still will be," James said, "but keep a good heart, my lass!"

"If all I hear about going on snow-shoes is true, then it's a good balance I'll need besides a good heart!" Kate laughed.

James and Davie made snow-shoes for them. They bent willow twigs into a shape something like a tennis-racket, and strengthened the centre with narrow pieces of wood, then they laced strips of buffalo hide from side to side to hold the pieces in place. The shoes were fastened to the feet by thongs of animal skin, leaving the heels free to lift a little.

Kirsty tried a few steps on the flat ground round the camp.

"It's like skating on snow. It's fun! I like it!" she cried.

"Try going up that bank," Davie told her. There was a hint of mischief in his voice. Kirsty took up his challenge.

"Watch out! Dinna dig your shoes in like that!" Davie shouted.

The warning came too late. The front of the shoes tripped Kirsty up and she fell head over heels in the snow. "I—I canna get up!" she cried, the snow shoes waving madly in the air. "I canna get standing!"

Davie roared with laughter. "I *knew* that would happen!"

"Then it was awful mean of you to tell me to do it!" Kirsty said indignantly. "Give me a hand!"

"You've got to practise going up and down hill, you

know. It will not be level ground here all the way to York Factory." Davie helped her up.

"I would never have got on my feet again if you had not been here."

"Oh, yes, you would! You just roll over and take your snow-shoes off," Davie told her.

Kate and Kirsty practised hard, and when the end of March came the whole family were judged fit to go with the advance party to York Factory. Robert Finlay came from Fort Churchill with Indian hunters and guides, and on April 6, 1814, the brave party set out. Donald Gunn the piper went ahead, his plaid flying in the wind, his bagpipes skirling the old Scottish songs to encourage the folk behind him. After him came Archibald McDonald, the leader, Mr. Finlay and a guide. The men came after him, pulling their belongings and provisions on sledges, then the women, and at the rear came one or two of the stronger settlers to help any stragglers.

It was a hard terrible journey, for they had to keep going through all the hours of daylight. Every morning at three o'clock they were wakened by a gun-shot. The first morning Kirsty was terrified.

"Whatever's that? Are we being attacked?"

"No, Kirsty! That's Mr. Finlay firing to tell us it's time to get up," Davie laughed.

"But it's black night!" Kirsty objected.

"It will be grey light by the time we've stripped the tents, rolled up the blankets, packed the sledges and had our breakfast," her father told her. "We've to push on as hard as we can in the hours of daylight."

Another gun-shot warned them when it was time to start. No one was ever late. They were always ready to start at the mustering post. Never was there a more enduring band of people. For nine days they kept going, pushing one weary foot in front of the other, hauling on the sledges, uphill and down-hill, along the ice of rivers to give smoother going wherever possible. Then one morning Kirsty sank down in the snow.

"I canna go on!"

"I wonder if I could carry you," Davie said doubtfully.

"Then ye'll have to carry me too, Davie, for I'm fair weary," his mother said. Other women in the party declared they could go no further without a rest. Davie ran ahead to warn Archibald McDonald and Mr. Finlay. They came hurrying back with him.

"We canna keep up the pace," the women told him.

"I've got cramp in my feet," one woman said. Others, too, had cramp and blistered heels. Mr. Finlay knew all about the pain of snow-shoe cramp.

"There is nothing to do but to call a halt," he agreed. "We will make a camp for you here and leave an Indian guide and hunter with you. The rest of us must press on to York Factory to bring food and help for you. We will leave you provisions for ten days, but if you are fit to travel before that time, make haste to follow the trail."

The very next day, however, some of the advance party returned.

"We've come on a store of birds the hunters from York Factory have left behind. There's plenty of meat and to spare, so we have brought back supplies to you."

With plenty of food to renew their strength and with rest for their blistered feet, the women soon recovered and were able to press on again. With shorter marches they reached York Factory only a few days behind the others. The ice on the rivers had not completely broken up, so they had to wait for a month at York Factory. This time, there was plenty of food, however, and the Company people treated them very kindly. There was music and singing and Highland dancing in the evenings, in which Davie and Kirsty played their part.

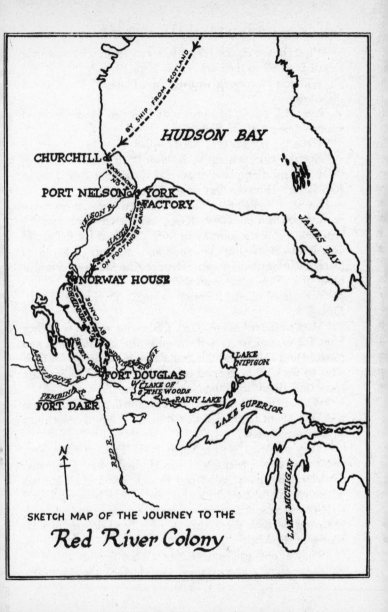

BY SHIP FROM SCOTLAND

HUDSON BAY

CHURCHILL

PORT NELSON · YORK FACTORY

NELSON R.

HAYES R.

JAMES BAY

ON FOOT AND BY CANOE

NORWAY HOUSE

BY CANOE

WINNIPEG R.

SEVEN OAKS

ASSINIBOINE R.

LAKE NIPIGON

FORT DOUGLAS

LAKE OF THE WOODS

RAINY LAKE

PEMBINA

FORT DAER

LAKE SUPERIOR

RED R.

N

LAKE MICHIGAN

SKETCH MAP OF THE JOURNEY TO THE

Red River Colony

At last the ice on the Hayes River melted and it was time to say farewell to their friends at York Factory.

"Will you be coming with us, Mr. Finlay?" Davie asked the trader.

"Aye, lad, I will. My post is at Brandon House, beyond your settlement at the Forks."

"What are the Forks?" Kirsty asked.

"Not the kind you eat with, lassie!" the trader laughed. "It is the meeting-place of several rivers that run into the Red River. There's a fort there, Fort Douglas."

It was a tremendous moment when the canoes were pushed out into the Hayes River and the settlers began the last long leg of the journey to their promised land. Donald Gunn was in the leading canoe and the skirl of his pipes lifted their hearts. To their surprise, the children found a band of Indians going with them.

"Are the Indians friendly to us?" Davie asked Mr. Finlay.

"Most of the tribes are. They trade with us, you see. They hunt for us and we give them guns and ammunitions and tobacco and knives and things like that in exchange for their furs, so we kind of depend on each other. The Indians are more our friends than the Norwesters are."

"Who are the Norwesters?" Davie asked. "I heard traders speaking about them at Fort Churchill. They did not seem to like them much."

"They are men of the North West Trading Company, rivals and sworn enemies of the Hudson's Bay Company. They employ many half-breed French and Indian hunters whom we call the Bois Brulés, because of their brown colour."

Kirsty shrank at first from the fierce-looking Indians with the paint on their faces, their feather head-dresses and the knives in their belts.

"They'll not eat you, Kirsty! They're very good to children. Here comes Peguis, the chief of the Saulteaux

Indians. He is a great friend of the white people. Hi, Peguis!" he cried.

"How, Finlay!" the chief said solemnly, holding up his hand in greeting.

"Here is a lad who wishes to be a hunter, Peguis." Mr. Finlay thrust Davie forward.

"How!" said the chief, extending a hand. "Shake!"

Davie shook hands with the big chief.

"You fire gun?" Peguis asked.

"Yes, I can shoot," Davie answered eagerly. "Mr. Finlay taught me."

"Good! And squaw-child?" He pointed to Kirsty. "She make moccasin?"

Kirsty shook her head. The chief shook his head too. "Bad! All squaw make moccasin."

"She can make mitts," Davie said, holding up his fur mitten. "She made these."

This time the chief nodded approval. Kirsty stared fascinated at his feather head-dress. "You like it?" Peguis asked with pride.

"It's beautiful!" Kirsty said in admiration.

Solemnly Peguis took off his head-dress and detached a feather. He gave it to Kirsty, pointing to the cap she wore. Kirsty fished in her pocket and brought out a safety pin and fastened the feather in position.

"That gift is a token of friendship and a very great honour, Kirsty," Mr. Finlay told her. "Have you any small thing you can give Peguis? The Indians like a gift in return."

Kirsty looked troubled. "I've only another safety pin." She took it from her pocket. "It seems a foolish kind of gift."

"Just the thing! Peguis will be pleased indeed with that."

Kirsty shyly offered it to the big Indian.

"Good! Good!" Peguis was tremendously pleased with

the safety pin and fastened it in his tunic like a brooch. He put out a hand to Kirsty. "Friend? Shake!"

Kirsty's fear of him melted away. "Friend! Shake!" she said, putting her hand in the chief's big one. The friendship with Peguis was to mean a great deal to all of them in the days that lay ahead.

On May 23 the Sutherlanders began their seven-hundred-mile trek by canoe and on foot. At first the banks of the Hayes River were low and the current slow, so canoeing was easy. Then the river banks rose steeply and the black water raced along through a narrow channel. Canoeing against the stream became hard work. The Indians set the pace and the Scots who wielded their paddles with them had hard work to keep up with their strokes. Peguis himself took Davie and Kirsty in hand and showed them how to turn the blade at the end of the stroke and to guide the direction of the canoe with it. Soon they reached waterfalls and rapids where the men had to lift the canoes out of the water, unpack them, and carry canoes and goods along the river bank till they reached smooth water again. This was called making a portage. An hour before sunset a camp was made on the river-bank, tents erected and a meal cooked over camp-fires, usually a stew made of partridges or wild geese, hares or rabbits, and occasionally a deer. A deer meant plenty of meat for everyone.

Only the men carried guns. Peguis noticed Davie's longing eyes on his gun.

"You not big enough yet," he said to Davie, who shook his head regretfully. "But you big enough for bow and arrow," Peguis remarked, touching the bow he carried across his back and the arrows in his belt.

"I've never shot with bow and arrow," Davie replied.

"You try?" Peguis unslung his bow and offered it to the boy.

"Show me, please," Davie said.

Every evening Davie had a practice with the bow and arrow.

"You stand like this." Peguis took up a stance. "Now fit the arrow. Look along arrow. You see what you want to hit? That tree? Now bring string back like this." The bow twanged and the arrow was quivering in the tree trunk. After that, every evening Davie had a practice with the bow and arrow while Peguis looked on. Often when a portage was to be made Davie carried Peguis's bow and arrows, to leave the Indian free to carry his canoe.

One day when a long and difficult portage had to be made, the children ran, as usual, along the bank beside the river. Sometimes Kirsty stopped to pick wild flowers that were springing up in the woods. This time a carpet of wild anemones tempted her from one glade to the next.

"Hi, Kirsty! Better not go too far into the woods! It will soon be sunset," Davie called as he followed her. Just then he caught the movement of horns behind a thicket.

"Ssh! Keep still! There's a deer there," he told Kirsty. "I'm going after it! It would be a feather in my cap indeed if I could shoot a deer for meat for us."

On stealthy feet they stalked the deer, twisting and turning among the forest glades. Somehow the animal always managed to keep a bush or trees between himself and his pursuers. At last he broke cover and bounded across an open space. Davie let fly with his arrow. It was a beautiful clean shot which hit the deer in the throat and brought it crashing to the ground.

"I've hit it!" Davie cried, rushing to examine the deer. "It's a clean kill!" he said with satisfaction. "There'll be venison for dinner to-morrow, Kirsty."

"It's too big an animal for us to drag back to camp, Davie."

"Aye, it is indeed! We'll have to get the men to carry it away. We must fetch them quickly. It will soon be dark."

Already the light was fading and a white mist was rolling up from the river.

"Which way do we go?" Kirsty asked.

Davie looked about him, perplexed. "I think we came that way. I remember that big pine tree."

"But there's another pine tree just like it over there," Kirsty pointed out.

The sinking sun shone redly between the massed tree trunks. Soon it would dip below the thick undergrowth of bushes. The river mist rolled nearer. Davie pointed to the lowering sun. "That must be roughly north-west. If we follow a line west of that we should come to the river and then we can follow the bank."

They struck out in a westerly direction, skirting clumps of bushes and crashing through foot-high grass. Thorns plucked at them and nettles stung them.

"Surely we did not come this way?" Kirsty said.

Davie was beginning to have his doubts too. "Perhaps we had better go back to the other pine tree," he said, when all at once they came on an open space. Beyond it rose a clump of rocks. "If we can get to those rocks and climb them, we might be able to see where we are." Davie took two or three steps forward, then he sank up to his ankles in soft spongy ground.

"Stay where you are, Kirsty! Don't move! It's a bog!" he cried, trying to pull out his feet. As fast as he pulled out one from the squelchy mud, the other seemed to sink in deeper, almost to his knees.

"I'm sinking!" he cried.

"What shall I do? What shall I do?" Kirsty was frantic.

Davie was still carrying Peguis's bow. "Catch hold of that and pull for all you're worth!" Kirsty hung on to a bush by the edge of the morass, leaned forward and grasped the end of the bow and pulled with all her strength. Davie managed to lift one foot out and struggle forward a step, then pull the other foot after him. Again he sank in the mud, but not so deeply this time before he lifted his other foot for the second step. Three more plunging steps and he was standing on the tussock of grass with Kirsty.

"My! That was a narrow escape!" He shuddered. Kirsty was trembling violently.

"We must go back the way we came," Davie said. "We can follow the path we've made through the undergrowth."

It seemed as if the bushes held out thorny hands to pull them back. The sun dipped below the horizon and the grey mist seeped through the forest, blotting out their surroundings. Soon they could not even discern their former tracks. They came to an open glade among the trees.

"Which way now?" Davie said desperately.

"We're lost! We're lost!" Kirsty lamented.

"Let's try that way." Davie pointed.

"No, no! I'm sure that will take us back to the bog. Oh, Davie, I'm so frightened. I dare not go on any more."

"Let's shout," Davie suggested. "Maybe the camp is not so far away and they'll hear us."

They lifted their voices again and again, but not even an echo answered them.

"They'll come and look for us when they find we're missing." Davie tried to sound more confident than he really felt. "We'll stay here where we can rest our backs against the trunk of this big tree."

They sank down beside it. The darkness began to creep around them. There was a rustling in the undergrowth. Kirsty sat bolt upright.

"Davie! There's something creeping among the bushes. Could it be a wolf?"

Davie knew it was quite possible, but he answered boldly, "Nonsense! It's more likely to be a rabbit."

"I wish we'd a fire," Kirsty said. "I'm so cold, and wild animals will not come near a fire, Peguis told me."

"It's clean daft I am!" Davie declared. "I've got a flint and tinder in my pocket after lighting the camp fire this morning. Feel round and see if you can find a bit of dry grass and some twigs."

Kirsty found a handful of withered reedy grass, and Davie, on his hands and knees, found dry cones beneath the pine tree. He struck away at his flint till a spark flew, and then another and the tinder caught alight. He touched the papery grass with it and a little flame shot up. He fed it with the fir cones and bits of brittle twigs. Soon he had a small steady fire glowing. "That feels better," he said.

Kirsty, her back firmly against the tree trunk, glanced nervously round the encircling forest. In the darkness among the bushes she saw something gleaming. She clutched her brother.

"Davie, there are eyes watching us from those bushes, not just one pair, either! There must be animals there, perhaps wolves, waiting, waiting—"

Davie saw them too. He lit a large twig in the fire, then stood up and whirled it round his head till it glowed bright red, then he flung it with all his might and main among the bushes to which Kirsty had pointed. There was a plunging and rustling in the undergrowth and the gleaming points of light vanished.

"They're gone, but they'll come back again," Kirsty said in a frightened whisper. "What shall we do, Davie? They'll tear us to pieces."

"Keep the fire going!" Davie said. "Here's a thick dead branch, like a small tree trunk. It's too thick to break but we can keep pushing an end of it into the fire as it burns. I'm going to find more wood."

"Oh, Davie, don't leave the fire! The wolves might get you!" Kirsty cried in terror.

"I shall take fire with me," Davie said, lighting another small branch and waving it about his head. He searched at the base of other nearby trees and came back several times with an armful of dead twigs and branches. "Perhaps these will keep us going till daylight," he said. "Daylight comes early in this country."

"What if we fall asleep and the fire dies down?" Kirsty said fearfully.

"We wust not fall asleep. We must sing to keep ourselves awake," Davie decided. "We'll sing together at first, then each in turn, as we used to do when we looked after the herd at Culmailie."

Suddenly Kirsty's voice rang out in the well-known words of the twenty-third psalm.

> "The Lord's my Shepherd. I'll not want.
> He makes me down to lie."

As they sang, they both felt comforted.

At the camp, when it was found just at sunset that the two children were missing, the search began. James Murray thought Davie might have gone fishing along the river and he and Mr. Finlay tramped along the bank, searching and calling. They returned to the camp dismayed. Robert Finlay sought out Peguis.

"We think the two children belonging to Mr. Murray must be in the forest."

"I go look for them," Peguis said at once. "I take Indian hunter with me."

"We had better take lanterns," Finlay said. He, too, thought of the wolves that might be roaming the forest and shuddered to think what might have happened to the children. Each man took a lantern lit with oil made from animal fat. Peguis also brought one of his hunting dogs. "Give dog something to smell belong squaw-child," he said to James Murray. Kate brought out a pair of Kirsty's moccasins from the tent and the dog smelt them, then cast around for a while along the river bank, then seemed to pick up a trail that led to the forest. Peguis followed the trail as keenly as the dog, noting bent grasses here, a broken twig there, a couple of flowers that had fallen from the bunch that Kirsty had picked. The trail wandered through the woods till, all at once, the dog gave a bark and bounded forward. A still shape lay across their path. James Murray gave a cry of fear, but the still figure proved to be the body of the deer Davie had shot. Already beasts of prey had been at its carcase. In its throat the arrow was still sticking. "My arrow! The boy shot it," said Peguis.

The trail led them to the edge of the morass where they found trampled footmarks on the muddy bank. Peguis held James Murray back. "Not good go there. Man sink!" He pointed to the marsh.

"Have my children been swallowed up in the bog?" James cried in agony.

"No! I read the marks. Feet go in a little way, the boy's, but feet come out. It is plain. They go back to the forest." Suddenly Peguis flung his head back. "I smell smoke!" He sniffed around. "That way!" The dog was straining at the thong which held him.

They plunged back into the forest, crashing through the undergrowth. Suddenly the big chief stopped and help up his hand for silence.

"Listen!" he said. From among the trees came the faint sounds of a Highland Jacobite song, "Will ye no' come back again?" sung by two very tired voices. Peguis hesitated no longer but broke into a run. A minute or two later they came on the two children crouched by their sinking fire.

"Kirsty! Davie! I wondered if I'd find ye alive!" James Murray said as he ran to them.

"I *knew* you'd find us, Father," Davie said in a trusting weary voice.

"It was Peguis found you. He followed your tracks through the forest to the morass. He knew you were not in the mud there and turned us back."

Kirsty held out a hand to Peguis. "Dear Peguis!" she said, the tears beginning to fall.

"Give me the squaw-child," Peguis said. "I carry her back to camp." With infinite tenderness the Indian gathered her into his arms and the bobbing lanterns led the glad procession back to the waiting camp and Kate.

7. THE MASSACRE AT SEVEN OAKS

AFTER travelling twenty-nine days the Sutherlanders reached the forks of the Red River where they were to make their new homes. Here on a long point of land, where the Red River took a bend to its meeting with the Assiniboine River, the first settlers in the New Colony had already built their wooden houses. Behind the settlement stretched hundreds of miles of rolling prairie lands.

"Where are the mountains?" Kate cried in some disappointment. James, however, looked pleased.

"This is far better land for farming than mountains. This land has deep good soil for crops, and grass in plenty for the animals."

"It is a good wide river too, with plenty of fish," Davie said with satisfaction.

"Here is the Governor, Miles MacDonell, and the first settlers, waiting to welcome you," Robert Finlay told his company.

Every settler carried a musket in his hand. At a sign from the Governor, each man raised his musket and fired a salute of welcome in the air.

Willing hands helped them ashore. There were shouts of greeting, for many of the Sutherlanders had relations among the settlers already there. Miles MacDonell shook hands with every person as they came up the river bank. A sturdily-built man clad in deer-skin trousers and jacket ran forward. "Hullo, there, Robert Finlay!"

"Why it's Peter Fidler! What are you doing here?"

"Mapping and parcelling out the ground for Lord Selkirk's settlers. I'm making sure every man gets his hundred acres. I never did a job with a better heart. I'll give you a hand with your gear."

"Help this bundle of liveliness with her blankets, first," Finlay laughed, pointing to Kirsty. "Came on snowshoes she did, from Fort Churchill to York Factory, the youngest one of us to make that tough journey!"

"Well done, little lass!" Peter Fidler said in a voice which still had a pronounced Derbyshire accent.

"And this young man has every promise of being a good hunter. He's a fine fisherman already, so you'd better give him a piece of land right on the river bank."

"I'll try to do that," Peter Fidler laughed.

"And here are James Murray and Mistress Murray. Mr. Fidler is the surveyor and map maker to the Hudson's Bay Company."

They shook hands all round and Peter Fidler eyed the Sutherlanders with approval. "Know anything of farming, Mr. Murray?"

"Aye, I was a crofter back hame in Scotland."

"You will find it grand farming soil here," Peter Fidler assured him. "But come this way now, for Governor MacDonell is waiting to welcome you."

Miles MacDonell made them a speech of welcome. Food and drink were handed round, then came the more serious business. Governor MacDonell handed out a musket and ammunition to every man.

"Our first care must be the protection of our colony," the Governor told the settlers; "I warn you, you will find we have enemies among the Norwesters. You will also need to hunt for your meat. The Indians will supply us with buffalo meat and pemmican, but it may not be enough."

Davie lined up with the men who were receiving the guns. The Governor paused when he saw him. "Why, you're but a lad!" he said, holding back the musket.

"He is a good shot, that same laddie!" Robert Finlay said quietly.

"He make good hunter," came the deep voice of Peguis from behind the group.

"If we are attacked by the Norwesters, we shall need all the good gun-men we can muster," Peter Fidler remarked.

The Governor hesitated no longer. "Here's your gun then, lad, but see you make good use of it and keep it clean and in good order."

Davie glowed with pride as he received the shining new weapon.

Next, to each family the Governor gave an Indian horse, a bag of seed potatoes, and wheat, barley and turnip seed.

"And now Mr. Peter Fidler will show every man his hundred acres of land," the Governor announced. "Every family is to have a farm by the river. The fishing of the river is free to you too."

"Fishing!" Davie exclaimed with delight. "We'll have to build a boat, Father."

"The house and the land will come first," James informed him sternly. He turned to the Governor. "Please, sir, where do we get our implements, ploughs and harrows and spades?"

The Governor looked rather uncomfortable. "I am sorry to say that these have not been sent out to the colony yet. They will come in time. Meanwhile there is a supply of hoes and one or two spades, but that is the best we can do."

Peter Fidler brought out his plans and showed the colonists where their new homes were to be.

That night Donald Gunn played his pipes and the Highlanders held a great party with singing and dancing. Davie sat alongside Peter Fidler, and while they were watching a Highland reel he put a question that had been in his mind all day.

"Mr. Fidler, what did you mean by saying that if we were attacked by the Norwesters we should need all our gun-men?"

Peter Fidler looked serious at once. "There has been a lot of enmity between the Hudson's Bay Company and the North West Company. We both trade over the same country with the Indians for furs, you see. Then it is a question of the buffalo herds too."

"The buffalo herds?"

"Aye, laddie. The longer you live in the northlands the more you'll learn that everything hangs on the question of *food*. Men of the same blood will kill each other for meat. We depend on the buffaloes for dried meat for winter. The prairies round here are their chief grazing grounds. The Norwesters fear that the settlers making farms here will drive them away, or else the colony will require all the buffalo meat in the territory. Indeed, they're right about that."

"Would it not be better to have farms with herds of cattle on which men could depend?"

"Aye, lad, you've got some sense there, but it will be a long time before the settlers get their herds flourishing, and meantime you've all got to eat. Miles MacDonell knows if the settlers are to live through a hard winter they cannot spare any food to the Norwesters. He has forbidden the Norwesters to take any meat out of the Colony lands, either by killing buffalo or trading with the Indians for their dried meat. The Norwesters will not submit to that and there has been trouble already."

"What kind of trouble, Mr. Fidler?" James Murray was sitting near, and he heard what the surveyor had told Davie.

"Well, the Norwesters' hunters, the Bois Brulés, have stolen some of our cattle. Then, when our settlers go out to hunt the buffalo, the Bois Brulés make the herds stampede. Then, early this year, the Governor learned that big supplies of pemmican and dried meat had been taken out of the Colony lands to Fort La Souris, belonging to the Norwesters.

He sent some men from Fort Douglas in this colony to raid the fort and they brought away thirty tons of supplies."

"Thirty tons!" Davie let out a whistle of surprise.

"Aye, that might prevent death by starvation of the colonists, but you may be sure the Norwesters will not let it rest there. They will seek their revenge."

"We seem to have arrived in the middle of a small war," James Murray remarked.

"Aye, man! Now you can see why the Governor was willing to supply Davie here with a musket."

The next day the Sutherlanders said goodbye to Robert Finlay who was going on to Brandon House, another Hudson's Bay Company post; then they set to work at once to build their new homes, felling trees to make log huts. The men worked in teams, helping each other. Meanwhile, the women were busy with spades and hoes, took off the turf and dug the soil and planted potatoes. Kirsty worked alongside Kate, and whenever Davie could be spared from housebuilding he dug and planted with them. What time could be spared from building and planting, Davie spent fishing in the river from the bank at the foot of their land. It was a hard life, but they were all happy in it.

"Better this than the life in Glasgow!" James said. "Here a man can earn his bread like a man!"

Kirsty had marked off a plot for herself and was making a garden. She planted wild roses and prairie poppies and other field flowers in it. "I've always wanted a garden," she said, "and Mr. Fidler says he'll give me seed from England that he had sent out to him, wallflowers and pinks and lavender."

"Here I am making a home again," Kate said with gladness, as she and James added piece after piece of furniture made with their own hands.

By the time the winter came the Sutherlanders were well settled in their comfortable huts. Their first crops had yielded well, especially the potatoes and turnips. The trouble with the Norwesters, though, was building up.

Miles MacDonell had to go away from the colony to deal with an attack on Fort Daer, another of the Company's posts, and while he was absent the Norwesters made a camp at Frog Plain, three miles north of the settlement, not far from the camp of Peguis and his Indians. The leader of the Norwesters, Duncan Cameron, tried to persuade the Indians to join with him against the colonists. Peguis shook his head. "Among these people I have my friends," he told Cameron. "It is a bad thing for a man to take up weapons against his friends." The faithful Indian could not be moved.

It was difficult for the Sutherlanders to defend their farms when the men were working in the fields, and often a band of the Bois Brulés made a raid on their homesteads, broke open the byres and drove off the cattle and plundered the houses.

One day in June when James Murray was helping another settler to fell trees some distance away, a band of Bois Brulés rode up to the Murrays' farm and drove away the cow which was pastured in a field near the farm. For the cow James Murray had paid most of his savings. It was their dearest possession and meant milk and butter and cheese for them. Davie and Kirsty saw what happened from where they were working in the vegetable garden.

"They shall not get away with it!" Davie cried in anger.

The horse was stabled next to the house, and Davie dashed in to it, carrying saddle and bridle. Kirsty went with him and helped him to fasten the girths, and when Davie mounted the horse she climbed up behind him and held on to his belt.

"Better get down, Kirsty! I'm going after our cow and there'll be rough men to deal with, and perhaps shooting," Davie told her.

"They'll be less likely to shoot if there's a girl with you on the horse," Kirsty said, sounding a lot braver than she felt, but she was determined not to let Davie go alone.

"*Will* you get down, Kirsty?" Davie besought her.

"I will *not*! If you do not want to lose our cow for good, then you will waste no time getting after the thieves, Davie Murray!"

Davie was forced to ride away with Kirsty clinging round his middle. He urged the hardy Indian horse as fast as it would go. He knew the cattle thieves could not go faster than the pace of the cattle they had stolen and that he could catch up with them. There was a cloud of dust ahead as the raiders drove the cattle, towards the Norwesters' encampment. The thieves had to pass the Indian camp as they went. Peguis watched them with an unmoved stare till a few minutes afterwards when Davie and Kirsty went galloping past. This time Peguis was moved to action. "Bring my horse!" he called to his son.

Davie and Kirsty caught up with the raiders just as they were turning into the encampment.

"Hi, there! Give us back our cow!" Davie challenged them.

"What cow?" the leader said with a sneer when he saw he had only two children with whom to reckon.

"That cow!" Kirsty pointed to the animal. "She's Rosie, *our* cow!"

The leader burst into a scornful laugh. "How can you prove she is your cow?"

"She is! She is!" Kirsty insisted.

"Not any longer!" the leader sneered. "You children had better get back home if you don't want to be made prisoners along with the cow."

"If I had my gun with me, you would not speak to us so!" Davie cried angrily.

"Oh! Got a gun, have you?" said one of the Bois Brulés. "So you'd threaten us? I think perhaps such a dangerous

135

fellow should be taken prisoner. His horse would be useful to us. Get down, both of you! Your sister can walk back by herself."

"I will not!" Kirsty kicked out at them when they made to lift her from the horse.

"Looks like we're going to have two prisoners on our hands," the leader said. "I wonder what ransom the settlers would pay to have her returned to them unhurt? They think a lot of their women."

Kirsty realised with horror the trap into which she had fallen. The enemy would use her in bargaining against her people. "Let me go! Let me go!" she cried wildly as they came once more towards her.

"Do not touch the squaw-child!" came a stern voice from behind the crowd. It came from Peguis, mounted on his horse, with his son on another one beside him. Both held drawn bows with the deadly arrows fixed. "The first man who touches the white child shall have my arrow through his heart!" he declared.

The Bois Brulés knew that at that distance Peguis could not miss. One by one they stepped back from the two children on horseback.

"Which is their cow?" the Indian chief demanded.

"There she is!" Davie cried, pointing out Rosie.

"Drive that cow away from the others!" Peguis ordered.

"Are you going to obey an Indian?" the leader asked the Norwesters. "Will you let *him* tell you what to do? What would two be against the lot of us, if we rushed at them?"

The situation looked ugly, but the Indians never flinched. The hands that held the bows remained steady as ever.

"We should not be two against you," Peguis told the leader. "Kill us and all our tribe will come against you. They will come silently in the night. You will know nothing till you feel knives at your throats. Are one cow and two Indians worth that vengeance?"

The thieves drew back and muttered among themselves. "He is right! Let the children go, Pierre," the Bois Brulés urged their leader. "What are the children worth to us?"

Pierre saw the temper of the crowd was against him. No man wanted Peguis's arrow through his heart. "Be gone with you!" he shouted at Davie.

"Not unless I take our cow too!" Davie said, holding his ground.

There was a rope dangling from Rosie's neck by which the men had pulled her along. Suddenly Kirsty slipped down from the horse and boldly seized the rope. "I will lead her back!" she said.

The Bois Brulés were too astonished to make a move. Davie was quick to urge his horse between Kirsty and the cattle thieves. "On with you, Kirsty!" he cried.

"The first man who goes after them gets my arrow through his throat!" Peguis declared, sitting still as a rock. Not till Davie and Kirsty were hidden from view behind the bank of a creek did he relax his grip on the bow. He looked at the thieves with contempt. "I did not know that *men* made war against a *squaw-child*!" Then, without a backward glance, he and his son rode away back to the Indian encampment.

Affairs went from bad to worse between the settlers and the Norwesters. The Norwesters got a warrant for the arrest of Governor MacDonell for breaking into Fort La Souris and carrying off their supplies of meat. MacDonell sent back a message of defiance. Then, on June 10, when night had fallen, the Norwesters fired on the settlement, wounding two men. This seemed like open war. They then sent another message to say that if MacDonell would give himself up and stand his trial, the Norwesters would leave the settlers alone. MacDonell called the settlers to him.

"My people, I am going to surrender in the hope that it will save further bloodshed among the colony. The Norwesters can take me to Montreal and I will stand my trial there."

"I do not think it will save the Colony, sir. The Norwesters mean to wipe us out altogether," one of the older settlers said.

"Aye, I fear it, but perhaps my surrender will give you a breathing space," MacDonell decided.

The old settler was right. Nothing but the destruction of the colony would satisfy the Norwesters. Four days later they attacked the settlers' houses and carried off some of the men as prisoners. The rest of the settlers gathered at Fort Douglas for greater safety, taking their wounded with them. The women and children took refuge behind the inner walls: the men, James and Davie among them, stood at doors and windows with their muskets primed. There came a hail of bullets against the walls of the fort, but little damage was done.

"We will show them we are not defenceless!" John McLeod, a settler, said. "Haul out our cannon!"

"It is rusty, and it is a long time since it was fired," a man told him. "We have no shot for it, either."

"Could we not use chain-shot?" James Murray suggested. "If we break up the chains on our carts they will serve as shot." The blacksmith went to work at once, snapping off the links of chain.

The Bois Brulés were massing behind a screen of bushes, ready to make an onslaught on the stockade around the fort. Just as they broke out, yelling murderously, McLeod gave the order "Fire!"

The cannon roared like a thunderbolt, sending the pieces of chain screaming about their ears. Taken by surprise, the Bois Brulés halted abruptly, their horses whinneying and rearing; then some turned tail altogether and made off as fast as they could. The rest were soon in retreat.

"First victory to us! They'll come back again, though,"

McLeod said soberly. "We cannot hope to stand against them for long, only sixty of us, men, women and children. There are nigh on three hundred men of them, and what pity will those brutes have for our women and children and wounded?"

"What do you think we should do?" James Murray asked.

"I think we must abandon the settlement. There is little food in the fort and they could soon starve us out. They have drawn off now, but they will come back to-morrow night and they might try to burn us out. We had better use to-night to get down the river to Lake Winnipeg and Norway House. Get the canoes ready and embark the women and children and wounded. We will take what gear we can, blankets and clothes and food. The cattle we shall have to leave behind. There is no room for herds in the boats."

A bitter sigh went up from the colonists. Their cows and sheep meant the savings from many months' labour.

Dawn saw the boats well down the river. By the time the Norwesters crept up to ambush the fort again, the settlers were many miles away. When the Norwesters found the colony was deserted, they burned the settlers' homes, broke down the fences, trampled the growing crops into the earth and carried off the cattle.

"We have knocked the colony on the head!" the Norwesters chanted; but they had not succeeded in turning out *all* the settlers. In the blacksmith's shop at the fort four determined men, among them John McLeod, barricaded themselves in with the little cannon pointing at the enemy. Each time any of the Norwesters tried to approach, they turned a withering fire upon them.

"Let them be!" the Norwester leader decided. "There are not enough of them to cause us any trouble."

Those four grim-faced men, feeding pieces of chain into

their cannon, stood for the indomitable spirit of the colonists.

It was a sad and dismayed band that made their way along Lake Winnipeg towards Norway House and the Jack River, once again to be their place of refuge.

"Is there to be no peace for us? Must we always see our home destroyed?" Kate said heavily.

"We shall go back again, you will see, Mother," Davie told her. "Perhaps sooner than you think!"

"Aye, we shall go back. I have not tilled my fields to give them up at the first breath of gunfire," James Murray declared.

Though they did not know it, already help was on the way to the settlers. Colin Robertson, a leader appointed by the Earl of Selkirk, reached the encamped settlers at Jack River. With him Robertson had twenty trained and armed men.

"Go back with me, good folk! Go back with me to your homes and build them up again. What is there here for you in this rocky barren place? At the Red River the land is yours, already tilled. Some of your crops may have been spared. If you go back, you will be in time to harvest them."

"What if the Norwesters attack us again?" one settler asked.

"This time there are more of us with guns, and ninety more settlers are on their way to us across the sea, coming with the Earl of Selkirk himself. Would you have the Earl come, and none of his people there to greet him?"

James Murray spoke up. "I will go back for one, and I think I can answer for my family."

"Yes, I will go!" Kate said at once, and Kirsty looked at Davie and nodded when he nodded. Other settlers followed their example. A few days later Colin Robertson led them back to the Red River colony.

When their canoes came to rest at the banks of the river,

the four remaining defenders rushed down to meet them.

"We knew you'd come back!" John McLeod cried with joy. "The Norwesters have left us alone for a while. Ye'll find we've looked after your farms as well as we could. We've repaired the fences and some of your houses, and we've tended the crops and made hay. Aye, and we've even started to build a new fort in the place of the one that was burned down."

The colonists went to look at what remained of their homes. The Murrays' log hut had been burned down, but the byre remained.

"We shall soon build it again, lass," James told his wife. "Meantime we must be thankful for shelter in the byre."

"My garden's been spared. The flowers are coming into bloom," Kirsty exclaimed with delight.

Kate smiled at Kirsty's joy. "Aye, whiles it takes longer to make a garden than to build a house."

That year the harvest was good, with oats, wheat, barley and potatoes in abundance. There was a second crop of hay cut and stacked. The new fort was completed. Many more settlers from Kildonan arrived from York Factory under the leadership of Peter Fidler, who also brought a herd of cattle and pigs in the canoes! With the new settlers came a new Governor, appointed by the Earl of Selkirk, Robert Semple.

Large herds of buffalo had been taken on the prairies, and plenty of cat-fish caught in the river and then dried, so there were stores of meat and fish enough to see everyone through the winter.

On November 4 they held a feast to celebrate the re-establishment of the colony. Amid much laughter John McLeod fired the cannon once more, this time in a salute as the flag was hoisted on the new fort. Everyone drank everyone else's health, and there was music and dancing, and Donald Gunn's pipes skirled far into the night.

The winter passed peacefully with the tending of cows and sheep. There was much visiting among the settlers, with singing and story-telling in the long winter evenings. There were even several weddings. All seemed set fair at last for the Red River Colony. Among the Norwesters, though, trouble was still brewing, ready to spill over in hate for the Hudson's Bay Company and the settlers at the Forks of the Red River. The Norwesters were not yet defeated.

The next spring the Norwesters got an army together. Again they tried to get the Indians to join them, but Peguis refused. On June 17, 1816, he came to see Governor Semple.

"Chief Semple, I bring you bad news," Peguis told him. "The North West men mean war against you. They come to Indians and say, 'The settlers drive away the buffalo and this make the Indians poor and miserable, but Norwesters will drive the settlers away. If the settlers fight, the ground shall be drenched with their blood. Not one shall be spared.' They ask that the Indian young men shall fight on their side."

Semple's face grew grave. "And what have the Indians said to this, Peguis?"

"We no fight our friends in the colony," the chief replied staunchly.

Semple shook hands with him. "I trust you, Peguis."

"There is more bad news," Peguis went on. "North West men have stopped your boats bringing pemmican. They have sunk them and taken your men prisoners. They have attacked Brandon House belonging to the Hudson's Bay people and have taken prisoners and steal everything. Now they come your way."

This was shocking news indeed. "How many men, Peguis?" Semple asked

"I hold up my hands seven times," Peguis said, showing his extended fingers.

"Seventy men! That's a big number, Peguis."

"Too many bad men for Red River people to fight," Peguis replied. "They make themselves to look like Indians, but no men of my tribe among them, Chief Semple."

"I believe you," the Governor said. "Thank you for bringing me this news, Chief Peguis." They shook hands.

"Keep a watch, Chief Semple. My young men say the Bois Brulés attack you in two days."

As Peguis rode away he passed by the Murrays' farm and beckoned Davie who was working in the fields. "You have good eyes, boy? You can see long way?"

"Yes, I guess so. Why, Peguis?"

"Norwesters come soon to colony. You go Governor Semple and tell him I think you good boy to keep watch from tower at fort."

When Davie told Semple what Peguis had said, the Governor replied, "I trust Peguis's judgement in many things. Go, take up your duty at Fort Douglas at once and keep a sharp watch, lad. You had better take my spy glass."

"Can my sister Kirsty come with me too?" Davie asked. "She has very sharp eyes."

"Aye, two watchers might be better than one," Semple agreed.

The settlers were warned of the threatened attack and mothers and children came to stay in Fort Douglas for better safety. The men stayed on their farms to look after the cattle and crops.

A day went past but nothing happened, and neither Davie nor Kirsty had seen any movement of troops across the wide prairie, though they kept the spy-glass shifting in all directions. At night their father took over from them, but all was quiet, with only the wind rippling the prairie grasses. Then came the day when Peguis had thought the attack might come. For several hours all seemed quiet. Some of the settlers went to look after their cattle in the fields by the river bank. Still Davie and Kirsty kept careful watch. Suddenly Kirsty said, "What is that little cloud of dust over there on the horizon, Davie?"

Davie took the spy glass from her instantly. "They're coming!" he cried. "Horsemen heading this way! I must warn Mr. Semple at once!"

He ran down the stairs and broke in on the Governor, who was snatching a hasty meal. "The Norwesters are coming, sir! A great crowd of them on horseback! They look to be about three miles away."

Semple jumped up at once. "Go back and keep watch, and shout down to us behind the barricades if they change direction at all." He dashed away to look at his defences.

In the fort there was anxiety and fear. Mothers with small children wept: men shouted directions to man the barricades. The cannon was brought out again. All seemed excitement and confusion, but Semple kept his head. Davie called to him from the window.

"Mr. Semple! There are still settlers with the cattle in the river fields. They cannot have heard the alarm. The Norwesters are headed in their direction. They'll cut off our settlers before they can reach the fort."

"We must go out and meet our enemies," the Governor decided. "I want one man from each family to go with me."

A number of men volunteered immediately, James Murray among them.

The enemy were mustering their horses by a clump of oak trees known as Seven Oaks when Governor Semple and his brave band approached. Semple halted half way. "There are far more Norwesters than I thought," he said. "John Bourke, go back and fetch out the cannon and bring with you another twenty volunteers."

They waited a few minutes, then Governor Semple decided to go forward.

"We will see if we can settle this thing peaceably," he

said. They advanced towards the clump of trees where the horsemen were gathered.

"They've tricked themselves out in Indian war-paint. They mean to fight," one of the colonists said.

Grant, the commander of the Norwesters, divided his forces in two and swung half of them in behind Semple, while the other half advanced towards him. A Norwester called Boucher rode forward.

"What do you want?" he demanded roughly of the Governor.

"What do you want yourselves? These are our lands," Semple shouted back.

"You have destroyed our fort," the Norwester accused him. He was speaking of Fort Gibraltar which the Hudson's Bay people had attacked. "You are a rascal!" he told the Governor.

Semple retorted, "Scoundrel, do *you* tell *me* so?" He seized Boucher's bridle with one hand and caught hold of the man's gun with the other. Boucher jumped from his horse and made to strike Semple. At that moment, in a panic, one of Semple's men fired. At once gunmen replied from the Norwesters' side, and Holte, Semple's lieutenant, fell by his side. Both sides began firing as fast as they could.

A small crowd with Davie, Kirsty and Kate, watched from the tower of Fort Douglas. They heard the shot fired, and saw the Norwesters raise their guns to their shoulders and fire a volley in reply.

"Oh!" Kirsty cried. "They're killing our men!"

"Mr. Semple's shot!" Davie cried. "He's not killed, though. He's lifting himself on his elbow."

"Father's fallen!" Kirsty cried in horror-struck tones. "He's lying on the ground!"

White to the lips, Davie turned the spy-glass on his father. "He—he's not killed, Kirsty. I saw him lift a hand just now. He's on his hands and knees and crawling towards the river.

Oh, a body of men has come between us and I cannot see him any more!"

A new horror caught Davie's eye. "The Norwesters are rushing at them now, firing left and right as they go. There's a man standing over Mr. Semple with a pistol in his hand! He's shot him through the chest as he lies wounded. Oh, the wicked murderers!"

"Where is your father? Can you see him yet?" Kate cried in agony.

"No, I cannot see him. There are so many bodies lying on the ground." Davie gave a groan. "Oh they're killing the wounded with knives and pistols! They're sparing no one!"

"Oh, Father! Father!" Kirsty wept.

"James! James!" Kate moaned, then slumped on the floor in a dead faint. Kirsty rushed to help her.

Just then there came a shout from below. "Bourke is taking out the cannon. Every man stand by to defend the gates!"

Davie seized his gun and rushed to the stockade. Bourke had mounted his cannon on the bank and fired in the direction of the enemy. His shot fell short, but the sight and sound of the cannon made the Norwesters draw off from killing the wounded. Six men escaped from the field of battle and came running towards the fort, only six of the twenty-eight that had gone out with Semple. James Murray was not among them.

8. THE LAND OF PROMISE

THE enemy did not advance at once as the settlers had expected, but drew off to meet the other half of their army and to make plans to attack the fort next day. All night the men in Fort Douglas stood to arms, waiting for the onslaught. About midnight a sentry was hailed by a quiet voice from some bushes on the other side of the fort away from the Norwesters.

"Hi, white men! Peguis wishes to speak with you. Open your gate to him."

"We shall not open our gates. How do we know you are Peguis?"

"Do not shoot. I have news for you. I will come in close to the palisade to talk to you."

"This may be a trick to draw us away from the side where the Norwesters might attack," the sentry said to his fellow-watchers.

Davie was standing on guard too. "If it is Peguis, we had better listen to what he says. He has always been our friend," Davie observed.

"Go to Sheriff MacDonell and ask him to come here, Davie," the sentry instructed him. Sheriff MacDonell, a relation of Miles MacDonell, was leader now that Semple was dead. MacDonell agreed to go to the river gate and speak with Peguis. Davie went with him.

"We have found a wounded man lying among the rushes of the river. His eyes are closed and he cannot speak, but he still breathes," Peguis said. "If you will open the gate when we call out to you, we will carry him into the fort."

"How do we know this is not a trick to get us to open the gate?"

"It is Peguis speaking. Peguis not lie to white men."

"I really believe it is Peguis speaking, sir," Davie told MacDonell.

"Suppose Peguis has gone over to the enemy?"

"Peguis? Never!" Davie declared with conviction.

"Is there a lad called Davie there?" the Indian asked.

"Yes, I am here, Peguis."

"Send the boy out to Peguis, and Peguis prove he speak truth."

"Let me go, sir! Let me go, please!"

MacDonell hesitated. "It might be a trick of the Norwesters to get a hostage, Davie."

"No, Mr. MacDonell! They could have taken hostages among the wounded instead of killing them," Davie said bitterly. "What good would a lad like me be for a hostage? Let me go to Peguis, sir. If you will place a ladder, I will climb over the palisade, and then you would have no need to open the gate."

MacDonell ordered a ladder to be brought and Davie mounted it.

"Stand by to catch me, Peguis," he called softly.

There was a rustling in the darkness below the high fence. Davie drew a deep breath, then jumped in the direction of the sounds. He was caught by ready hands before he touched the ground.

"Peguis?" he said.

"Ssh!" Peguis placed a finger on Davie's lips. "The Norwesters not far away. Come!"

Davie followed the shadowy figures to the river bank, sometimes crawling over the ground so they should not be sighted by the enemy. On the bank, with an Indian crouching beside him, a figure was lying. Davie sank down beside him. "Father?" he whispered.

It was James Murray, sure enough! For a terrible moment Davie thought he was dead, and he whispered,

"Father! Father!" again, more urgently. James Murray stirred a little and opened his eyes.

"Father, it's Davie here, with Peguis."

"Davie?" James voice was faint and bewildered. "Davie? Where are we?"

"Ssh! Peguis found you unconscious. You've been wounded."

Recollection came back to James Murray. "My shoulder!" His hand went up to it. His shirt and coat were drenched in blood. "I crawled behind the bushes to the river," he muttered.

"He's lost much blood," Peguis said. "He very weak. We carry him to gate of fort."

One of the Indians hoisted James Murray over his shoulder, and the little band crept round the bushes, stopping now and again behind cover to make sure they had not been observed by the Norwesters. At last they reached the fort. Davie called softly through the gate, "Is Mr. MacDonell there?"

"Aye, I'm here, lad, waiting," came the reply.

"It is no trick; Peguis found my father wounded by the river. The Indians have brought him in. I beg you to open the gate."

In a few minutes the great battens that held the gate closed were removed and one side of the gate swung open. Like shadows, without a word, the Indians carried in James Murray and set him down. Peguis gave MacDonell and Davie a brief handshake, and slipped through the gate again. Like shadows still, the Indians vanished into the night.

While careful hands placed James Murray on a stretcher, Davie rushed into the tower to tell his mother.

"Mother! Mother! Father isn't killed after all. He's sore wounded, but Peguis has brought him in."

Kate's hand went to her heart. She could hardly speak.

"He's below in the courtyard," Davie went on.

Kate was suddenly stabbed into life again. "Come with me, Kirsty!" she cried and sped down the steps.

James was sorely wounded, but it was found that the bullet had passed clean through his shoulder and out at the other side, so there was no need for the doctor to probe for the bullet. With the hole plugged and bandaged, he lay on a straw bed within the fort, trying to swallow the hot milk that Kirsty brought for him. The colour came back a little into his cheeks.

"Given a day or two to rest, and plenty to drink, he'll soon make up the loss of blood," the doctor promised.

"Will any of us get any rest?" MacDonell asked in a low voice. "To-morrow the rascals will attack us for sure!"

Cuthbert Grant, the commander of the Norwesters, was ashamed of the way his men had slain the wounded on the field of battle. He knew, too, that if he attacked Fort Douglas and harm befell the women and children there, the vengeance of the Hudson's Bay Company would be swift and terrible and it would fall upon him. It would be better if he could persuade the colonists to abandon the fort peacefully. The Norwesters had taken one prisoner, John Pritchard. Grant sent for him.

"You have seen what happened on the battle-field, that we gave no quarter," Grant said to him.

"There was no mercy shown," Pritchard replied in a quiet voice that brought the colour of shame to Grant's face.

"I promise you that if there is any further resistance from the garrison at Fort Douglas, neither man, woman nor child shall be spared." Grant told him in a terrible voice.

"Is there no means by which the women and children could be saved?" Pritchard implored him.

"I will spare their lives if the colonists will surrender the fort to me. I will allow them to go away in peace and give them an escort past the Bois Brulés on their way up the river. They must give up everything in the colony. You can take these terms to Sheriff MacDonell, John Pritchard."

Under guard, Pritchard was taken to the gate of the fort, to carry this message to MacDonell. When the Sheriff heard the terms, he was wild with rage.

"What? Give up all we have striven and worked for here for more than five years? Give up all our homes and farms? Grant asks too much. We will not surrender."

"MacDonell, think what will happen if you do not agree?" Pritchard begged him. "Grant has said he will spare neither man, woman nor child. Think of the women and children and what might happen to them at the hands of those half-savages. Is it not too great a price to pay? The Norwesters outnumber us both in men and weapons. Sooner or later they will take the fort. They threaten to fire it and roast alive all in it.

MacDonell shuddered. Pritchard pressed home his argument.

"Grant has promised he will let you all go in peace, provided there is no resistance. Is it not better to live and take our families to safety, so that we may yet fight another day? Lord Selkirk himself is already on his way to bring help to the colony."

"Very well. You can tell Cuthbert Grant we will surrender," the Sheriff agreed with a heavy heart.

It was a pitiful procession of settlers that wound its way down to the canoes by the river bank. They were only allowed to take with them the clothes they stood up in, their blankets, and food for the journey. As they reached the canoes they were roughly searched for valuables or documents. Many of the men were questioned.

James Murray's bandages were hidden under his tightly buttoned coat. He had recovered enough to be able to walk. Kate held his arm, pretending to lean on it herself as they passed the searchers. Just as they reached the canoes, they were stopped.

"I'll look at the inside pockets of your coat, man," a searcher said.

It might have gone ill for James, but just then a shout went up, "There's Bourke! The man who fired the cannon at us! Get hold of him and place him in irons!"

The searcher ran to help in his capture of Bourke. The Murrays stepped quickly down into their canoe and Davie pushed off at once from the bank. Even as they paddled downstream, the smoke from the settlers' burning houses rose behind them. Frightened and bewildered, the settlers left their Red River colony for the second time for the Jack River. Nothing was left to them of their colony but the bodies of a score of brave men lying on the ground by the oak trees. In the dead of night, when the Norwesters had departed, Peguis and his Indians went to bury the men who had been their friends.

At Jack River the settlers gave themselves over to despair.

"Let us go back to Scotland!" was the cry of most of them. "Let us ask the Hudson's Bay Company to send us a ship to take us home again."

Almost to his own surprise, James Murray spoke against this.

"What is there in Scotland for us now?" he asked. "We shall yet make homes in this new country if you have courage enough."

"What is the use of building houses to have them burned down by the Norwesters every time?" one man asked.

To her own surprise too, Kate found herself siding with James. "Were not your homes burned in Scotland?" she asked. "Who is to say it could not happen again there?" Suddenly the look of the one with 'the sight' came into her eyes. "I tell you that even yet this land will be a land of promise for us all, a land flowing with milk and honey."

"I would rather have the promise of a ship to take us away," a settler sneered. "I say, let us all go to York Factory to wait for any ship that might come."

"You had better stay where you are," an officer of the Hudson's Bay Company advised them. "You will be worse off if you have to winter on the shores of Hudson's Bay."

They decided to build huts and stay by the Jack River, but never had they spent such a miserable winter. They were short of food and clothing. They had to catch white fish through holes they made in the ice. Now and again they got supplies of pemmican and rice from Norway House. With the coming of spring, however, hope began to lift in their hearts again.

"Maybe we'll get back yet to the Red River in time for me to plant my garden," Kirsty said.

Suddenly, in the middle of March, great news came for them. A man of the Hudson's Bay Company arrived at the Camp.

"Good news, folk! Take heart! Miles MacDonell and a company of soldiers have taken Fort Douglas back from the Norwesters!"

An eager crowd surrounded him, asking questions.

"Aye, it's true enough," he told them. "Ye'll be able to start back right away."

"But will the Norwesters come down on us again?" someone asked.

"If they do, there'll be a warm welcome waiting for them! Lord Selkirk is bringing a company of soldiers with him, a small army who've seen service abroad. They're to have land at the Red River too, in return for protecting us all."

A loud cheer went up from the colonists.

"Well, folk, what will ye do now? Ask for a ship, or go back to the Red River?" the official asked.

"Go back! Go back to the colony and our farms!" most people cried.

"What shall *we* do, Kate?" James asked.

She did not hesitate. "We have come so far on this journey, James, that it is as far to go back as to go on. We'll make our home at the colony again."

"And you, Kirsty?"

"I'd like to plant my garden and see it bloom."

"And you, Davie?"

"The Red River was a grand place for fishing and—and I'd like to see Peguis again."

Though the ice was still on the rivers, the colonists travelled back. As soon as the frost had gone from the ground they set to work to dig and plant potatoes and barley and wheat. There was little food in the colony, but Peguis and his Saulteaux Indians hunted for them, and even dragged meat to them on sledges. The soldiers worked alongside the settlers and built homes for themselves too, and planted fields. The Norwesters knew they could never hope to turn out the settlers for a third time, and they left them in peace, save for stealing an occasional cow.

On June 18, 1817, Lord Selkirk arrived at the Forks to visit the colony. A great feast was held at Fort Douglas to which the Indians of the Cree and Saulteaux and Assiniboine tribes were invited. Among them was Peguis. A tremendous 'pow-wow' began.

"We come here in peace to be your friends and neighbours," Lord Selkirk told the Indians. "I thank you for the protection and help you have so faithfully given to my people. Especially do I thank Peguis, the Chief of the Saulteaux Indians, who has been the friend of the colony and to whom many of us owe a debt that can never be repaid."

There was a tremendous burst of cheering at this. The old chief rose to his majestic height and spoke in reply.

"Great Silver Chief!" he addressed Lord Selkirk. "We have seen with sorrow the sufferings of your people. The Saulteaux tribe has always been your friends. I hold out to you the hand of friendship now, and I ask you to smoke the pipe of peace with me."

Lord Selkirk and Peguis shook hands, then the long pipe was puffed ceremoniously by Peguis and then by Lord Selkirk. Then it was passed from hand to hand, everyone in the circle taking a puff or two at it. Davie was standing immediately behind his friend Peguis. To his surprise Peguis passed the pipe over his shoulder. Davie took his ceremonial two puffs, then returned the pipe to Peguis.

"You handed that pipe back right quickly!" Kirsty teased him.

"You be glad you're a girl and that you were not asked to smoke it!" Davie retorted.

"Another puff and you'd have been sick!" Kirsty jeered.

"You would have been sick at the first puff, my lassie!"

After the pow-wow with the Indians was over, Selkirk announced his plans for the colony.

"For you who lost your houses and crops and animals when the enemy came upon you, I give a free grant of land of one hundred acres each, fronting on the Red River below Fort Douglas. Peter Fidler will show each of you where your lands are situated. These lands shall be yours and your heirs for ever."

Another cheer rose from the settlers.

"Hear me further!" Lord Selkirk said, holding up his hand for silence. "On this ground where we are met to-day shall be built a church and a home for your minister. The land on the other side of the creek shall be for your school, with a house for your school-master. In memory of the lands you have left in Scotland, I name this parish Kildonan."

"Kildonan!" the Sutherlanders cried in joy. "Kildonan!" There was hardly an eye in which the tears were not bright.

That evening James and Kate Murray, with Davie and Kirsty, sat on the river bank.

"A grand place for a fishing boat, Father!" Davie remarked with a twinkle in his eye.

"Aye, after you have both finished building our home!" Kirsty reminded them with a laugh.

"This will be the place for my garden, on this bank sloping to the sun," Kirsty said happily.

"On this great wide prairie we can grow our corn and raise our flocks and herds," James dreamed.

"Already I can see the corn stretching golden to the west as far as eye can see." Kate said, her eyes rapt as one who sees a vision. "This will be the end of our journey, James."

"Aye, and a hard desperate journey it has been, my lass, but we have won through at last."

There was silence for a few minutes as they all thought of the long way they had come, then Davie asked, "What shall we call our new home?"

"I know!" Kirsty said. "So that we shall remember Scotland in this new land, and that the old and the new are bound together for ever for us, let us call it Culmailie."

"Aye, Culmailie it shall be," James Murray agreed.

Also available in Kelpies
by Kathleen Fidler

The Droving Lad
Escape in Darkness
Haki the Shetland Pony
Seal Story
Turk the Border Collie

If you enjoyed this Kelpie and would like a **free**
Kelpie sticker and catalogue please write to us
at the following address:

Canongate Kelpies
Canongate Books Ltd
14 High Street
Edinburgh EH1 1TE

GET A KICK FROM A KELPIE